First in My Heart

A Novel

Rachel Blanchard

1

Ava's stomach dropped along with the aircraft as Central Florida spread out in front of her. Row upon row of houses sporting meticulously manicured lawns crowded her vision. Glistening lakes slashed through the landscape every so often as if to remind visitors that nature still had a forceful presence there. The view was breathtaking, but it couldn't be more different than the golden fields that she had left behind. She couldn't help but think, *Am I making the right choice?*

Moving cross-country to work at a girl's clothing store was not a logical step in Ava's life plan, and it was almost as if she was planning a trip for another person when her fingers mechanically clicked open the email: "Transfer Positions Available in Hydrangea's Newest Location: Summer Shores, Florida." She got that same automated feeling when her zombie-travel-guide self searched up area schools, confirming that, although it was January, Summer Shores still had a few pages worth of teaching positions available.

Even a master organizer like Ava couldn't pull off a move that big only two weeks after her winter graduation, so she decided to wait and make arrangements to move down in May instead. Transferring her familiar retail job to the same town that she had contacts in seemed like a comfortable enough situation to give Ava the chance to explore the schools that she might want to work at long-term. Surely she would find the perfect place to teach in. God wouldn't have presented her with a life-changing opportunity—unlike any risk she had taken before in her life—only to let her fail upon arrival. *Would he?*

Ava's musings were brought to a halt as the plane landed, her doubts ultimately swept away with the bustle of passengers grabbing their bags and keeping track of their children. She hunkered down in her window seat to wait out the crowd, shooting a text message to Jess to let her know she had arrived. Her friend felt it necessary to convey the depth of her excitement by replying with five distinct emojis.

Feeling every bit of her tourist status, Ava checked and triple-checked every sign directing her first to a shuttle, then through a terminal, down an escalator and into the baggage claim. Just as she had found the carousel designated for her flight, she heard a shout.

"Ava!" Jess Wilson's tight dark curls bounced as she ran toward her friend.

"Jess," Ava croaked, striving for air after being nearly toppled by Jess's embrace. Her attacker's grin was infectious as always. Though small on the outside, Jess's energy more than made up for her size. "It's so good to see you," Ava finished. Jess steered Ava back toward her husband, who was waiting with a little more dignity a few feet back.

Ava pulled him in for a hug. "Isaac, how are you doing?"

"Oh, you know, hanging in there!" Isaac's easygoing nature was a great complement to his wife's exuberance. Ava hadn't seen her classmates much since high school, and not at all since they moved down from Iowa two years ago, but their familiarity was balm to her frazzled nerves.

Something else had changed in the Wilson household—Ava noted a tiny arm curled around Isaac's leg and fell into the grown-up's customary vice of ignoring everything else when a baby enters the scene.

"Hey, Noah," Ava called softly. She waved to no avail.

When his mother echoed his name and Noah peeked out, Ava hardly felt that "baby" was an appropriate term for him anymore.

"Hi buddy, I'm your mommy's friend Ava." She leaned toward Jess. "How old is he?"

"One," Jess replied, shaking her head. "I know, I can't believe it either. He's walking and starting to talk. Time goes by so fast."

"Well, I'm glad I'm here now and I won't have to miss another moment!"

Noah only acknowledged the newcomer's presence with sideward glances, but these slight tokens gave Ava hope that he would warm up to her soon. With the help of some cereal snacks, he endured the wait at the conveyor belt nobly. An eternity later, Ava spotted her single purple suitcase on the baggage carousel.

"Packing light, that's not like you," Jess laughed.

"A lot of things have changed since you left," Ava hefted her luggage down. "But you might not think I'm so reformed once you see how many clothes I fit in here. I had to sit on it for a few minutes to get the zipper closed."

"I see."

"Seriously though, thank you both so much for letting me crash until I get on my feet. My mom and dad send their love–I know they feel a lot better about me coming since I'm staying with you."

Jess waved their concern away. "I miss them too! You tell them you're going to love it here."

"We're happy to have you," Isaac said over his shoulder, leading the way to the car.

Jess continued, "I'm assuming that, due to your valiant packing effort, you'll need to make a trip to the store soon?" Ava nodded. "We can get that done tomorrow, and then Sunday is church–we've been going to this place for a few weeks now, and I really think you'll like it. Plus, there are quite a few young men in the congregation..."

"Jess, are you starting in on her already? The girl just got here!" Isaac's playful reprimand held no bite, only affection, and Ava found herself noting, somewhat wistfully, that he and Jess were the perfect match. *Will I ever find that?* she wondered.

At the ripe old age of twenty-three, Ava knew that she had no room to sound so fatalistic, but when everyone around her was enjoying conjugal bliss, she couldn't help but feel the absence in her own life. Nevertheless, feelings were only feelings; experience had taught her to proceed more carefully.

"I think I need some time to recover from my last 'few young men,'" Ava looked pointedly at Jess.

"Those guys weren't right for you. They're just water under the

3

bridge. Water... that flows into a pond with lots and lots of fish!"

"Jess, really, don't." Part of Ava wanted to join in the revelry, but the other part stamped down the urge. It hurt too much to let hope grow, only to realize that it was all for nothing. "Men just aren't ready to commit, and I'm not ready for their unreadiness." Isaac cleared his throat and Ava amended, "People aren't ready. Men and women. Not many exist that you can actually count on."

Jess stabbed Ava's chest with a finger. "That outlook is way too cynical for a gorgeous twenty-something like you." Ava avoided an eye-roll that she knew would launch Jess into a self-confidence pep talk. *But seriously,* she thought, *if I'm such a catch, why did every man I've ever dated make his excuses and leave?*

She and her high-school sweetheart went out for three years before he informed her that he just didn't think long-distance would be possible. That, followed by some vague excuse about "needing more time for himself," made her realize that what he really needed more time for was picking up girls at parties.

He told her again and again how amazing she was while breaking up with her. She supposed it meant something that he cared enough about her to attempt to salvage her feelings. The string of casual dates that she had been on during college hadn't turned out much better. This time, she'd be more careful about who she let close.

Seeing that her speech was falling on deaf ears, Jess threw her hands up. "All right, I promise to be good from here on out." She crossed her heart. "No more plotting."

"Thank you," Ava sighed.

"Imagining, dreaming, drawing hearts around you in my mind, but no more plotting."

"You're hopeless."

The slight woman wrapped her arm around the tall, slender one. "And you wouldn't love me any other way."

In the Wilson minivan, the pair swapped stories about family and work. Jess pointed out the substantial Summer Shores Hospital building as they exited the highway, merging onto a grid of neighborhood streets.

Although the name Summer Shores capitalized on its proximity to the ocean, the nearest beach was an hour away. Nevertheless, the city gleamed with all the appeal of a tourist attraction. Old buildings in the heart of town were refurbished and accented with twinkle-lit palm trees. The place was bursting with contradictions, where outdoor cafes and mom-and-pop places cozied up next to retail outlets and office space. When the brick roads turned into residential pavement, the tropical greenery was replaced by more traditional oak trees. What was novel was the Spanish moss draped over their curving branches, transforming the street beneath into an enchanted archway.

"Oh," Ava eloquently remarked. After they exited the natural tunnel, the most striking scene was the painted sky overhead. She found herself wondering, *Have I ever really seen a sunset before?* Now, from witnessing Summer Shores, she realized that Ashwood's hills had burdened her vision of golds and lavenders, blush, and blue. Here the sky seemed to extend out forever in every direction.

"Helloo, Earth to Ava?" Jess called. Ava shook her head, a bit sheepish to have been caught so deep in thought again. Her friend extended her arms like a parading ringleader as they pulled into her driveway. "We're here!"

"Jess, it's gorgeous." Consistent with the design of the surrounding condominiums, Jess's home was a spacious ground-level unit, painted in a pale blue, with grand windows on every side. "So... Floridian!"

"Thanks," Jess laughed.

Ava retrieved her suitcase from the trunk and rolled it down the long sidewalk into the home's entryway. Jess had cozily decorated the walls with inspirational sayings and farmhouse decor, integrating antiques with touches of metal to layer in a slight industrial feel. Jess followed Ava's gaze to the more modern pieces. "Had to throw something in here for Isaac too."

"And you did a great job," Isaac called from the kitchen.

Ava eyed a collection of pictures from Jess and Isaac's wedding, smiling as she saw herself in one. "You haven't put up any baby pictures?"

Jess pouted. "No. Noah keeps me too busy! Can you believe I've already had the pictures *and* the frames shipped here, and just haven't put them up yet?"

Knowing Jess, Ava believed it. But on a day off, she would have plenty of time to help her friend out.

Jess led Ava past the open-concept living and dining area and down a hallway to the guest bedroom.

"You'll have to sleep across the hall from the baby, but he's going to be very quiet, aren't you?" She looked warningly down at the child in her arms. His eyes were heavy from the car ride.

"Don't worry about that. I'm looking forward to it." Ava didn't dare to kiss Noah's little head, but sent him a flawless grin instead. "You and Auntie Ava are gonna be best friends."

Jess latched onto her adopted endearment. "Auntie Ava needs her rest now — she's had a long ride on the airplane. Do you want to take a bath?" All signs of sleep danced away from Noah's face and he started bouncing up and down, sending Jess into acrobatics to keep him in her arms. *Like mother like son*, Ava thought. "Ok, good," Jess said. "Let's show Auntie Ava the way."

During his bath, Ava enjoyed hearing Noah's gibberish, his squeals of delight, and his mother's squeals of surprise every time a particularly large splash seemed to meet its mark. Meanwhile, she explored her new room. Jess's more feminine tastes shined through in the lavender walls, the gray flowered bedspread, and the painting of a quaint cottage over a cherry wood dresser. This homey, albeit noisy, place to settle in after her afternoon of awakened senses left Ava more content than she imagined she would be before leaving home this morning. *Home.* Her happiness dampened a bit at the thought of the ones she had left behind. She dialed her mother, kicking her shoes off at the foot of the bed. *Comfy mattress,* she thought with satisfaction.

Renee picked up before the second ring. "Hello?"

"Hey Mom. I'm here."

"How was your trip?"

"Good. I had to put up with some snoring from the guy next to me, but other than that, it was fine." The sound of her mom's voice and her dad's T.V. program in the background made Ava's eyes prick with moisture. "I miss you already."

"Oh Ava, we miss you too."

She swallowed her tears and said, "Tomorrow I think I'm going to check out my new store. It's supposed to be close by here. I bet it's huge."

"That will be nice. How's the city?"

"Busier than home, but honestly, once we left the airport,

6

everything seemed more suburban than big-city. Still, there should be a lot to do!"

"That's wonderful. Are you getting all settled in?"

"Yes. Jess and Isaac are so great," Ava said. "They're even going to let me borrow Isaac's car while I work on getting everything switched over." She sighed. "Car shopping, that's another thing on the list."

"You'll get it all done. I know your friends are glad to see you again."

"Yeah, they don't have any family around here. I don't know if I would have been so brave to come down all alone. But I guess they've met a lot of new friends," she muttered, "and eligible bachelors."

"Oh, I want to hear all about that!" Renee said brightly. Ava could just picture her leaning forward on her maroon armchair.

"Nothing to tell. You'll be the first to know." She hoped her mother was catching her less-than-enthusiastic tone. But some things were uncontainable. Like the zeal of a perpetual matchmaker. *She and Jess should form a support group,* Ava thought wryly.

"Well, I'll let you rest. Thanks for calling, Ava."

"Love you, Mom."

"I love you too." The click seemed to embody the finality of their separation, and Ava made a mental note to stop personifying events into emotions. It was getting to be much too depressing. She unzipped her overstuffed suitcase and dug out a pajama set, makeup wipes, her toothbrush and floss sticks. The rest could wait until morning.

Despite her hygienic freshness and travel fatigue, Ava was not relishing the prospect of her first night in an unfamiliar bed. She crawled in and pulled the sheets up around her neck, wondering what the next few months could hold.

God, she prayed. *Thank You for bringing me safely all the way here. I think You must have opened this door for a reason. But I'm not completely sure what that reason is. Help me to see.* She fought a rising sense of panic as she imagined floundering so far from home. *Help me to find a teaching job. Or help me to be satisfied with Your will, whatever that may be.*

She pictured the understanding looks she would receive once she hightailed it back home, never able to truly "make it" on her own. No boyfriend, no career, no growth. She would rather they laugh in her face than to not be fazed at her failure. Ava was determined not to let

7

this opportunity go to waste. She *would* learn something. She *would* get better. She had no other choice.

2

The next day, Jess wanted to get some of Noah's energy out, so after some eggs, toast, and a few minutes of corralling swim diapers and pool floaties, Ava went with them to the community pool. When she stepped outside, heat hit her like a slap in the face. Sure, the temperature would get up to the 80s in an Iowa summer, but degrees were only something a person could feel, not that they could see and taste and, *Oh my goodness, am I sweating already?*

She turned to Jess. "This is May weather?"

"Late May." Jess shrugged. "You'll get used to it. Just stay inside or in the pool." She pointed a finger toward the community's center, just visible behind their house. Curved and tiled with a white and navy mosaic, the pool looked more like it belonged in a high-end resort than in a subdivision. Ava eyed the chaises and umbrellas scattered around its sides.

"Yeah, I think I can get used to *that!*"

Jess packed Noah into a stroller and the trio trudged through the hazy heat towards the sizeable oasis. Ava was surprised to see only two other families swimming. "Is it always this empty?" Ava asked.

Jess nodded. "We get spoiled having it around every day, I guess."

"Nice!"

Noah caught sight of the water and started squirming out of his stroller seat.

"Hold on," Jess laughed. "I'll have you ready in a minute!"

It was more like five to rub him down with sunscreen and outfit him in a pair of tiny dinosaur trunks with a matching swim shirt. The kicker was a little baseball hat, which had Mom and Auntie cooing and snapping pictures. The grin he flashed them when he landed in the cool water was like a shot of pure joy.

"You guys must have so much fun together," Ava said.

Jess gave Noah an extra squeeze. "It's the best. Every day he's up to something new! It can be pretty exhausting though."

Ava replied, "I bet," knowing that despite putting in long hours, "exhausted" was the last descriptor she would choose for her friend.

"Oh well," Jess said airily. "I can sleep when I'm retired and he's out of the house." She turned to Ava. "So how have things been with you?"

"I'm just happy to be here. Everything's so beautiful, and I get to hang out with you again so that's an added bonus!"

"Obviously."

Ava bit her bottom lip. "I just hope everything with my new job works out."

"It will! You loved working for Hydrangea back home, and you will love it here."

"It can't be too different, right?"

"Definitely not. And different isn't bad, Ava. I think it's just what you need," she paused to rest her wriggling infant on the pool's ledge. "A change of scenery to help you remember how amazing you are." This time Ava let the eye-roll loose, and Jess swatted her with a handful of water. "I'm serious!"

"Really, Jess, I'm good now. I love you for saying that though." Ava grinned as if to prove her point, and they refocused on the bouncing baby. She had come a long way since high school, where her insecurities almost swallowed her up. Jess had been there the whole time, an unfailing supporter. Ava's outlook was steadier now, as she more successfully kept sight of how valuable she was in God's eyes. What other people thought of her, or even at times what she thought of herself didn't matter as much as that. As she leaned her head back into the water and let the sun beat down on her face, it was impossible to be swept down into old doubts or fears. Noah's peals of laughter filled the air and her heart.

# # #

The trips to scope out the new work location and to the grocery

10

store made Ava feel more ready for the week ahead. She hadn't forgot any essentials in particular thanks to her supersized packing list, but needed more than travel-sized samples of shampoo and toothpaste to survive.

Sunday, standing in front of the bathroom mirror, Ava tried to tell herself that she had splurged on new makeup yesterday because she had thought it would be a fun outlet for Jess—who rarely got to go shopping anymore. It surely was not because of some ulterior motive that ran completely contrary to her resolve not to think about guys.

The uncharacteristically dramatic charcoal eyeshadow made her green eyes flash and she thought about rubbing it off before she told herself it was vain to keep obsessing over her appearance. Ava had already spent a half-hour fussing over her eggplant wrap dress, her shoe choice (metallic wedges), and how best to style her caramel-colored hair. She had swept it up in a half updo, trying to capture that delicate balance of looking casual but put-together.

When Ava slipped into the kitchen, Jess did not help the whole nervousness situation. Instead, she dropped a box of cereal mid-pour. "Ava, you look amazing!"

"I just want to make a good first impression," she said slowly, halfway considering turning tail and changing.

Jess tapped her lips innocently. "On who?"

Ava held a finger up. "You promised. I want to make a good impression on EVERYONE I meet today."

Jess's hands flew up in surrender. "Fine, I give up." Her expression said she had anything but given up, although she'd let the subject rest for now. It was only Ava's third day here, after all. There would be plenty of opportunity for meddling later. "Just relax. You'll see, everyone is so nice. And who doesn't love you? Just be your sweet self."

"Thanks."

Noah made an impatient noise from his highchair, evidently noticing his food was still missing.

"Sorry!" Jess promptly slapped his kiddie bowl down on his tray.

After breakfast, they piled in the van. Ava's seatmate looked dapper in a green button-down and khakis, complete with a teddy bear. Noah foiled all her attempts at engaging him in conversation, but his umber eyes stayed glued to Ava the whole twenty-minute drive. Watching the trees roll by through the window gave her a sense of peace as she and Isaac, Jess, and Noah rode in companionable silence to Summer Shores Church. Yesterday, Ava had seen Summer Shores Hospital, and today, Summer Shores Church—it made her think that every place in the city wanted to lay claim to the town's charming name.

The church was painted a bright white, modest but pretty in scale and architecture. They parked, and Ava picked up Jess's covered dish. An older gentleman held the door open for her with a friendly smile and pointed her in the direction of the dining area. She hurried to put the brownies down on a table with other desserts, as she could already hear voices lifting together in hymns. Jess and Noah were waiting for her outside the sanctuary, and they joined Isaac, who was spreading out toys in the back row of chairs. Ava was used to sitting in pews, but she found the church's hunter-green seats to be comfy.

Isaac handed her a hymnal open to "It is Well With My Soul," and she was thankful to know the tune well. Though she felt a little insecure, she joined in with her soft soprano and soon the lyrics were speaking to her heart. After a few songs, the pastor stepped forward and said a word of prayer. He looked to be around sixty, with a shock of white hair and an easy grin.

As he spoke on claiming God's blessings through faith and obedience, Pastor Thomas really made Ava feel as if she were Joshua the legendary leader, on his knees after a heartbreaking defeat. The minister read the verse, "And the Lord said unto Joshua, Get thee up; wherefore liest thou thus upon thy face?" flinging one hand up into the air and shouting for emphasis. This caused a few sleepers in the congregation to jump. He pointed right at the audience and said, "there is a time to stop praying, and a time to act."

Ava shifted in her seat. She had thought that when she finally acted —when she plucked up the courage to leave home—all feelings of being disconnected from her surroundings would melt away. And although everything in the building—from Jess wrangling Noah next to her, to the bouquet of fresh lilies at the front of the church, to the light flooding into the sanctuary—brought Ava a feeling of unexpected warmth, it was like she was still waiting for someone to tell her what to do with her own life. And she didn't know if that lost feeling would ever change.

Ava was embarrassed to find that her own thoughts had run loose for several minutes of the sermon. *When I get home I'll have to see if they post a recording online,* she told herself. Meanwhile, Pastor Thomas was bringing his passionate performance to a close. "And after he followed God's lead—" his fist closed, and his voice hushed to a near-whisper. "Victory."

Victory. Ava hoped that her story would end in the same way.

When Pastor Thomas stepped down from the pulpit, Ava felt as if she was waking up from a dream. His enthusiasm for the ancient story made her think that she ought to do better about studying the Old Testament in her own reading.

He closed service by blessing the food that they were soon to receive, and by asking for members to speak out any prayer requests. This seemed like a refreshing personal touch—that even with a congregation of a hundred or so, they all seemed invested in one another's lives.

After service, a grandmotherly lady in a bright yellow dress turned to greet Ava. Her stance was bowed and arthritic, but her hair was coifed, makeup done beautifully, as if she had no other care in the world but to show up for worship. Her whole face creased up with a radiant smile, like Ava had brought her a gift just for being there.

"Hi, I'm Elizabeth Allen," the woman said, extending her hand.

They shook. "Ava Keller. It's nice to meet you."

"It's nice to meet you too! Are you a friend of the Wilsons?"

"Yes, we all went to school together. I'm actually living with them for the summer."

"Wonderful! Well, we're so glad you're here today."

The pastor himself appeared next to Elizabeth. "Josiah Thomas," he said, and he gave Ava a firm handshake. She thought to herself that if this trend continued, she might end up with one very sore arm.

"I hope we didn't scare you away yet." Josiah said in a mock whisper, "This one's a real troublemaker." Elizabeth shook her head with a sainted expression.

"Don't believe a word that he says! Except for the part about us wanting you to stay. Are you staying for lunch?"

"I am!" Just then, a woman who seemed to be slightly older than Ava joined the welcoming committee. Ava had to appreciate the woman's sense of style–she wore classy red pumps and a belted dress.

She had pearls on her wrists and two small daughters under her arms. The eldest, a brunette who announced herself as Rosalie, did a twirl for Ava.

"Mommy braided our hair today—do you like it?"

Ava bent slightly to speak to the girls at their level. "You both look beautiful. How old are you, Rosalie?"

"Six, and my sister Ivy is three."

Ivy offered Ava a shy smile. Her plaits were flaxen gold, favoring her mother's coloring.

"Well, it's very nice to meet you both."

Amber, their mother, led Ava to a potluck lunch hosted in the high-ceilinged fellowship hall. Ava took stock of the wide room, as she didn't get a good look when she was rushing in with the brownies the first time. True to a city addicted to sunshine, windows that were nearly floor to ceiling covered the walls. Six tables for the food lined the wall opposite them, and several smaller round tables dotted the center of the room. Ava was glad; she always thought round tables made for easier conversation.

With Noah safely deposited in a booster seat next to his father, Jess joined her in the lunch line, whispering, "Everyone's super friendly, right?" Ava nodded in agreement.

"Wow!" Ava filled her plate with a bounty of fried chicken, fresh fruit, and berry cobbler. She had had homestyle cooking before, but here, there were new things to try like okra, collard greens, and grits. A beverage dispenser filled with sweet tea made her grateful she was in the South (she could never understand how her mother could sip hers plain).

They rejoined Isaac, who was deep in conversation with a man in a tan suit. The man glanced toward Amber, Rosalie, and Ivy for a moment as they came up behind Jess and Ava, and the fleeting look was so tender that Ava figured he must be Amber's husband.

"Mind if we sit here?" Amber asked out of sheer politeness, as Rosalie had already made herself comfortable next to her dad.

"Of course not!" Isaac answered.

"Thanks." Amber turned to Ava and said, "Jess mentioned last week that you'll be working at the new Hydrangea? That store is so adorable—we had one back in Texas."

14

"Really? You're from Texas?"

"Yep! Moved down seven years ago."

Ava realized that she had never answered Amber's question. "Yeah, I'm looking forward to going back to work. It's the best. The clothes are great, but it's even better to see how beautiful the girls feel when they get all dressed up in sparkles and tulle." She looked apologetically at Jess. "By the way, I should probably warn you that I'm going to come home every day covered with glitter."

Jess shrugged. "Hey, the more the better! I need a little girliness back in my life with two guys around."

Ava told Amber, "But eventually, I want to be an English teacher. I'm not really sure what grade yet. I like little kids, but I've also seen teachers form some great connections with older students."

Isaac paused from his conversation to interject, "Ava, you should talk to Pete. He's a second-grade teacher, and I've talked with him before about the education system here. He's a smart guy."

Amber's husband, Mr. Tan Suit, flashed a smile toward a group of people sitting at the next table over. "Don't let my brother hear you say that." Ava followed his gaze to a cacophony of boisterous laughter where a man, maybe thirty years old, was regaling five or six teenagers who crowded the small table elbow to elbow.

Ava eyed the entertainer of the group. That, she decided, must be Pete. He was stocky with glasses and a sandy goatee. More dressed-down than his brother in a red polo. *Hmm...* Ava thought. *From what his brother said about him, we probably won't get along.* Self-importance was one of humanity's most repugnant qualities in her book.

"I'd like to see you try and get a girlfriend!" she overheard a gangly boy cry.

"Listen," Pete said. "It's not that hard. All these girls are the same. You take her around one of these touristy places, buy her an ice cream, let her wear your feet out as she walks into every single store, and go home. That's all they want."

Pete must have felt Ava's gaze because he looked her way. Caught, she instantly broke eye contact and scrambled to look casual. *Nope,* she thought. *He and I will definitely* not *be getting along.*

# # #

After church, Pete drove to his apartment, ready to relax just like

15

any other Sunday afternoon, and came in to his brother sitting on the couch with his feet propped up on the beat-up coffee table. Pete made a mental note to get Jake's old key back from him. Just because Jake used to live with Pete before marrying Amber, did not mean he had the right to barge in any time he wanted. It had been, what, seven years since they had shared the apartment? *Seven years*, Pete thought, and shook his head. Nothing much had changed for him in that period of time.

"What are you doing, Pete?" Jake asked him.

"I'd like to watch some T.V., if you wouldn't mind getting off my couch..."

"No, I mean what are you *doing*? With your *life*? All you do is sit here, play softball, and go to work."

"That's the way I like it," Pete replied, his brother's intrusion forcing him to sit in an old armchair with a way worse view of the T.V. *Great*, he thought. *Now I'm going to get a crick in my neck.*

Jake threw his arm into the air. "Come on, man, there's a better way to live. Go out more. Find some people to talk to who aren't second-graders."

"Second-graders have some pretty great things to say." Pete would never admit that this empty room was starting to get under his skin. "Besides, I don't exactly see any girls lined up around the corner."

"I'm glad you mentioned that!"

Pete leaned back in his chair, "Here we go."

"I don't know if you noticed, but there was a good-looking girl at church today. Nice, too. Her name is Ava Keller, and she's a teacher like you."

"I know who she is," Pete grumbled. "You're not the first person to offer some 'helpful advice' to me in the last twelve hours."

"Really? If that's the case, then maybe you should start listening."

Pete began to scroll through his phone to prove how little Jake's words affected him. "Don't you have a family to get home to?"

Jake shrugged. "I'll leave in a minute. But this is important."

"I'm sorry to disappoint you, but I'm not interested in asking Ava out."

"What's wrong with this girl now?" Jake folded his arms. "You didn't like the way she walked? Were her teeth too straight?"

16

Pete actually thought Ava's smile was nice, but he didn't figure this was the best time to bring it up. He responded calmly, "I know the type. From out of town, looking to find an adventure. You think that you can get that out of her head, and before you know it... she'll be gone."

Jake's teasing tone softened. "You can't let Isabelle run your life forever."

"I'm speaking hypothetically."

"No, you're not," Jake said as he picked up his discarded suit jacket and stood up, seeing there was nothing else he could say. He paused at the door. "But Ava isn't Isabelle. And you should give her a chance."

With that, Jake left Pete alone with his unwelcome thoughts. *Almond-shaped green eyes. An endearing timidity. That purple dress.*

Why did his brother have to come poking his nose in where it didn't belong? Jake didn't have to remind Pete that he had found the perfect wife who he was blissfully happy with. Pete could see that with his own eyes every time the whole family got together. But, based on Pete's first disaster of a relationship and his lack of success with anyone thereafter, contented married life just didn't seem like a reality for him.

Pete was sure that Ava was a nice enough girl, but if she was looking for a relationship, she had another thing coming. He would be nice to her, that was all. If he could just keep his mind from running out of control and getting unsatisfied with the awesome life that he lived, it would be easy. Everyone had their problems, including Ava Keller. And he was sure that some idiosyncrasy of hers would come up and take her off his mind.

3

Ava pulled her newly borrowed silver sedan into Hydrangea's lot for orientation day one. *Jess and Isaac are lifesavers,* Ava thought for the umpteenth time this week. She popped out of the car and hoped her heels wouldn't be killing her too much by the end of the day. Sure, she might yet regret the scalloped-edged shoes and matching pencil skirt but, as she told Jess yesterday, first impressions were important.

The Summer Shores' Hydrangea was a larger location than in Ashwood, slightly taller than it was wide; however, the store's sign, written in pink script against light-gray brick, was the same.

Although Ava initially thought that the store's name sounded more like a high-end flower shop than a clothing boutique, after working there, she discovered how appropriate the title was for its merchandise. Hydrangea was known for its dresses, tutus, accessories, and shoes in hues of violet, azure, and pink. As an employee, she could always leave little girls feeling like the flowers they were, their bags filled with newfound treasures.

Everything looked ready for the grand opening, from the white banner flapping in the wind, to the fresh sod and bushes painstakingly put into place.

The store's interior décor was much like the location back in Ashwood—ash gray faux-wood floors, mirrors in ornate, gilded frames, fabric flowers, and pendant lighting. However, the feeling of a small-town shop that the Ashwood Hydrangea had created was somewhat lost in the newer building's expansiveness. Ava felt like the main aisle stretched on forever as she made her way past empty racks and stacked-up boxes to the registers, where a small group had already congregated.

A twinkling gold nametag identified the store manager, Jenny, whose friendly wave gave Ava the sense that she would be a warm, approachable type of leader instead of the superior sort. Ava released a breath she hadn't realized she was holding in and found a space next to a young woman whose loose raven waves cascaded down almost to her waist.

The girl turned with a broad smile and extended her hand. "Hi, I'm Mariana Reyes."

"Ava Keller, nice to meet you."

"Where are you from?"

"Ashwood, Iowa." Ava knew that Mariana's kind nod was likely concealing the thought, *Ashwood-where?* "It's in the eastern part of the state."

"Ah. I'm just from around here!"

"That's great. It seems to be kind of rare to be a local. Do you like it?"

"I wouldn't want to live anywhere else. That's why everyone else is moving in."

Ava laughed. "True. I was a sales associate in Ashwood and decided to transfer over."

Mariana's face lit up. "Maybe you can help me then. This is my first retail job, and I'm a little nervous about getting the hang of everything."

"I would love to." It was nice to already find someone so comfortable to talk to at work. "And you can tell me what all there is to do in this amazing downtown!"

Jess hadn't had time yet to give Ava the official-official grand tour, as she liked to call it, but Hydrangea was just a short walk away from all the action. Ava might as well start exploring on her own. Having lived in one place all her life prior to now, Ava found it slightly disorienting to be unfamiliar with a whole new network of streets, and be dependent on GPS for everything from breakfast to gas stations—even though Isaac and Jess had been more than accommodating.

Mariana replied with enthusiasm. "Sure, sounds good to me!" She seemed to be maybe eighteen, with a sweet sincerity that matched her age but a social ease which surpassed it.

Their conversation was cut short by Jenny's opening comments. Their manager was the picture of professionalism in a black pantsuit, clipboard in hand. "Good morning. I'm so glad to meet all of you." She sent a stack of papers around the room. "If you'll take a look at these schedules, you'll notice that there are two different options listed. Some of you are coming with a bit more experience from our sister stores and others will need cash wrap training, so you've been split up accordingly."

Ava took a copy and was relieved to see that she would be helping to stock the store for the next couple of days instead of going through training about the Hydrangea brand and how to work the register. She could complete transactions in her sleep, and often did dream of customer service situations after one too many late shifts. She would much rather make herself useful right away.

It turned out Ava's celebrating was a little premature, because upon closer examination, she saw that Jenny had assigned her to complete the most dreaded of all merchandise tasks—the jewelry display. As much as she typically enjoyed her days at Hydrangea, Ava discovered that it took all of her skill as a professional not to eye-twitch when a little dear would stick out her finger as she skipped past, tangling all the chains together and even sending a few necklaces flying off their pegs.

Still, Ava couldn't help but squeal a little after she found her designated work location and cut open a box of new merchandise. Sparkling posts, initial necklaces, floral headbands, and charm bracelets abounded, making Ava miss her youth. She thought, *Honestly, would it be so hard to create such adorable accessories for grown-up girls too?*

Ava heard a suppressed chuckle behind her and spun, kicking herself for not being more composed. All thoughts of composure fled from her mind, however, as she laid eyes on her mocker. With tanned, olive skin, wavy black hair, and a muscular build, this guy wrote the book on tall, dark, and handsome. And he was carrying a second box of accessories right toward Ava's station. *WOW.*

She stuck out her hand. "Ava Keller," she said, before realizing that his hands were already full. She casually withdrew her own and

20

smoothed down her skirt.

"Jackson Green." His face was all politeness, but Ava noticed a smile once again trying to break free at the corners of his mouth. "It's a pleasure to meet you, Ava."

Ava returned to the task at hand. Blessedly, the necklaces appeared to be in individual plastic baggies, so she didn't have to worry about untangling them. She opened and strung them up one by one on the turnstile.

Instrumental music switched on through the speakers and was pleasant at first, but Ava soon memorized the tones of the looped track. "The music is so much louder without people here, right?" she asked as Jackson worked on unfolding the headbands.

"Yeah," he said, "but I kind of miss the customers. It makes the day go by fast. Not—" he added "—that I'm having a bad time."

"I know what you mean," Ava answered. *In more ways than one.* "The customers will be here soon enough, and then we'll be so busy, we'll be looking for a calm moment."

"True," Jackson replied. "Though I can't imagine it'll be as busy here as it was at my last store in Iowa City."

Ava dropped the necklace she was hanging. So much for her righteous crusade on disrespected jewelry. "No way," she said, "that's the closest big city to me! I'm from Ashwood."

"Really?"

"Yeah. Small world. We could have even seen each other before." Although Ava doubted that she could forget a person like Jackson.

"My dad's the store manager over there. I guess it's only logical we're both from the same place since Hydrangea is just now moving out of the Midwest."

Jackson could call it logic if he wanted to, but to Ava, this was destiny. *Destiny, Ava? I thought you were going to take it slow...* Ava silenced the voice inside her as Jackson gave her a dazzling grin. Like seriously, the stuff of a toothpaste commercial. *Is this guy for real?*

But strangely, it seemed that he was. Their conversation was flowing in no time.

"Of course I thought that working in Florida would be fun, but my dream has always been to go overseas," he said. "There is so much need there. Once I save up enough to support myself, I'm going to find the right organization and really go make a difference."

"That's amazing," Ava shook her head. "Not many people are so selfless that they could put their whole life on hold for others."

"I don't really see it as putting my life on hold." He paused. "To me, it's giving my life meaning." He turned his gaze to Ava. "What about you?"

"I went to school to be a teacher."

"Teaching is a selfless job, too."

Ava squirmed. "I'm like you, I just want to help people. I'm going to do my best to do some good where I can. I mean, I student-taught in school, but until I find a full-time position, I won't be able to know if I can actually make it as a teacher." She sighed. "I wouldn't want to go overseas, though. What I've always dreamed about is settling down and having a family." She hoped that wasn't too personal to say.

Jackson put an assuring hand on her shoulder. "I think any school would be lucky to have you."

"Well, thanks." Ava stared fixedly at her hands, trying to tone down the blush burning up her cheeks. It wasn't working.

"Ava!" Salvation in the form of Mariana was headed Ava's way with a lunch bag and a thick paper packet.

Ava looked at her watch. 12:30 already. "That's my break. I guess I'll see you later!"

Jackson shook a box of hair ties playfully. "I'll hold you to that; we have a lot of work to do."

Mariana looked at him, then Ava with interest as Ava rose to meet her. The two walked to the employee break room, located behind the cash wrap. "It looks like you made a new friend," Mariana said cheerily.

"Yeah, I guess I did. How was your register training?"

Mariana's smile disappeared. "Overwhelming! I don't know how I'm going to keep all the keys straight, but I got some study material to take home tonight." She brandished her printouts.

"I felt the same way when I started. You'll get the hang of it. What do you have questions about?"

As they reviewed different transactions over lunch, Ava was reminded of why she wanted to be a teacher. Her heart sung when she saw Mariana's face brighten, like something had really clicked inside.

To make people's lives easier, to lighten their burdens—that was what she lived for. If only she could be capable to perform the job, to build up enough confidence to not get in her own way, she would succeed in the classroom just like she had learned to succeed in retail. Hopefully, by summer's end she would get the chance to try.

"Did you go to school around here?" Ava asked Mariana while munching on a turkey sandwich.

"Summer Shores High!"

"Is it a good school?"

Mariana saw where Ava was going with this line of questioning. "Yeah, I really liked it. But, just to warn you, there aren't usually a lot of openings. The teachers there stay there until retirement."

Ava exhaled. "Well I guess that's good—just not so good for me right now."

"I hope something works out for you. At least you have your job here."

"Thanks. I am happy about that. And I'm staying with my best friend and her family, so I'm in a good place."

Ava did have a great setup, but she would never truly feel at peace until she knew she was hired for a teaching position. She was really more of a planner than a fly-by-the-seat-of-your-pants type, and although her thoroughness could be useful when it came to things like organizing a fantastic display, it could also create undue anxiety.

"It will work out fine," Ava reassured both Mariana and herself. "So, what about you? Any big plans for the future?"

"I'm starting business school in the fall. I'd really like to work my way up to management, maybe even here."

"Hydrangea is a good company for it. They like to promote from within."

"I'm excited to get started!" Mariana bit her lip. "But maybe after some more practice."

"For sure!"

After their break, the boss unfortunately found Jackson and Ava's handiwork too efficient to require two people, so Jenny sent Jackson off to ink-tag tees. There was so much to do to get the store ready that the rest of the day passed quickly, and, before she knew it, Ava was headed back to her car. She nonchalantly looked around at the other

23

workers exiting, but Jackson was nowhere to be found. *Darn*, she thought, *he must have parked out back.*

Although the commute back to Jess's wasn't long, and Summer Shores couldn't rightly be considered a big city, the congestion at each stoplight was more than Ava was used to. She tapped her left foot impatiently and turned up the radio. She was a car singer—just not at stoplights.

It was a good thing that the light finally turned green, because Isaac subscribed to satellite radio, and they had a '90s station.

Belting out the songs she and Jess had danced to at every school party made her remember how carefree she used to be. As long as she had her friend by her side to laugh with, Ava could forget about all her fears. She thought that as she grew older, she would have more figured out, but it seemed that her challenges had only intensified.

Where to hang out on the weekends or whether or not she was going to finish that term paper was a far cry from buying a house, choosing a career, choosing a city, for that matter. She prayed that she could find her free spirit again. As a humble start, at the next stoplight, she didn't stop singing (though her shoulder-swaying decreased considerably).

She pulled in carefully to the Wilsons' two-car garage. Inside, Jess was sprinkling green onions over enchiladas, waving away Ava's protestations that she didn't have to cook for her all the time. The chef unsurprisingly sniffed out the boy news like a prized hunter and insisted on a complete description of Mr. Wonderful.

Ava couldn't help starting with Jackson's physical features. "He has light green eyes," she said, staring into the distance like a lovestruck teenager. "Dark hair. He's from Iowa. He wants to volunteer to help the less fortunate. And, he seemed totally into me." That last part was still baffling to her.

"He sounds perfect!"

"Yeah, maybe too perfect," Ava said, blowing out her breath. "I'm not going to lie to you and say that I'm not excited. But I don't want to get my hopes up."

"It's okay to hope for good things. You deserve it!"

"I don't want to tie my happiness too much to something that might go away. I'm going to try and take things slow and have realistic expectations." *Though that's easier said than done.* Their conversation was cut short as Isaac emerged out of the Wilsons' at-home office, logging off of his remote programming work just in time for dinner. Together, the four of them cleared out the whole cheesy pan.

While his mom was finishing up the dishes, little Noah surprisingly seemed to want to play with Ava. She was relieved her years of being a perpetual goofball were about pay off. She sang along with the television, danced, and narrated his surroundings like a theatrical performer until Jess said that it was time for him to calm down and go to bed.

"You can come with," Jess told Ava. "You're going to want to see this."

As her friend gathered Noah into her arms, Ava watched them warmly, but a bit wishfully. *I wonder if I'll ever have this*, she thought. There was just something about the way that Jess stroked Noah's head and held him tight that made his limbs go limp and his face relax. She spoke in hushed tones and gently carried him into his room. As soon as he hit the mattress, Noah curled up like a roly-poly bug and stuck his rear-end into the air.

Ava laughed and whispered, "That can't be comfortable. Is this how he always sleeps?"

"Every night." Jess looked so content that Ava had to give her a hug.

"I'm happy for you."

"You too. Just look at the two of us, together again! I'm so glad you're here."

Jess knew how to bring the lightness out of Ava, and it seemed in that moment that the only difference between past and present was that now, the two working girls had to cut their gushing and giggling short a little earlier.

4

Pete slammed his car door closed and trudged to the church entrance, weary to the bone. It wasn't always easy to come on a Wednesday night, but he was here. He was always here, and he figured that counted for something, tired or not. As he entered the fellowship hall, he couldn't help but be surprised at the sight of the church's newest visitor in animated conversation with Jon. That was one of the things he liked about the Summer Shores congregation—youth, adults, and elders all got along together. Pete took a seat as Jon, a teen not yet grown into his lanky limbs, asked Ava how her job was going.

"Things are going really well! We're just trying to get things ready for opening. I've already arranged to have Wednesdays and Sundays off so that I can be here from now on." At this, Pete raised his eyebrows, impressed and a little alarmed. So far, the image he had painted of Ava being noncommittal was not panning out. Even regular attendees couldn't always carve out time in the middle of the week for a church service. Still, he knew better than to put too much confidence in one person.

"That's great," Jon nodded before turning to clap Pete on the shoulder. "Pete, my man!"

"Hey, what's up," Pete said. He leaned over to shake Ava's hand and formally introduce himself. "Hi, Pete Harrison."

"Ava Keller," her small fingers fit in his for a moment before she drew her hand back to rest on her Bible.

Ava was eyeing Pete warily, reminding him of a skittish animal.

26

That's weird, he thought.

"Where do you work?" Pete asked, reaching for any subject. He was surprised he hadn't already gotten the info from Jake. He supposed he hadn't given his brother much opportunity to share.

"I'm working in a girl's clothing store called Hydrangea. Over on East Main Street?"

"Yeah, I noticed that going up."

"I transferred from the Hydrangea back home. I'm looking forward to it opening, but it should only be temporary until I find a teaching job. I hear you're a teacher?"

"Yep, second grade. Sorry, there's nothing that I know of open where I work, but it's only May. Something may come up."

"Yeah, if you could let me know if it does, I would appreciate it." She paused. "I'm not really sure what grade I want to teach. I'm certified K-12, so I guess I'll just see what comes my way. Do you like the second grade?"

"Yeah, at that age they still care about what you have to say. It probably has something to do with being awake." He ran a hand through his cropped hair. "You know, if you really want to know what group you like the best, you should come by and see what it's really like." *Great job, Pete. Let's spend more time with the girl that everyone is trying to set you up with.*

"Really? I will definitely take you up on that. I mostly worked with older kids in student teaching, and I need all the experience that I can get."

"School's almost out—you've got two more weeks to come by."

She pursed her lips. "I'd rather not plan anything next week since it's my first week of work—how about the Wednesday after next?"

"8:30, don't be late."

"I'll be there," she said, looking repelled by the mere suggestion of tardiness. She scribbled down the date and time in a paper planner. Pete was baffled. *Really, who still carries one of those around?*

She peeked back up at him for a moment, as if surprised that he was being so accommodating. He was irritated to think for a minute that he should have been friendlier on Sunday. A minute, before imagining being the type of person who ran around doing a song and dance around any person he might offend. *Nah,* he thought, *it's much better to*

27

be who you are and let anyone interested stick around. He could almost hear his brother telling him pointedly, "Sure, because you've had so much interest..."

Ava turned back to Jon. "I don't know," she sighed. "Everyone tells me I should be an elementary school teacher. But you can have great conversations with older students. I feel like I have a lot that I can share with them."

"Don't let anyone tell you what you can't do," Pete interjected. "Everyone told me I shouldn't do elementary. You seem like a capable person. You can do whatever you want."

"Oh, well...thanks. It's just, figuring out what I want is part of the problem."

"Sounds like you're doing something about it. You'll get there."

Ava nodded, unsure, as Pastor Thomas opened his Bible, indicating that the service was about to begin.

# # #

Ava left Bible study that night with her and Pete's conversation playing over in her mind. One note struck her in particular— "You can do anything you want." When Ava had first shared her desire to be a teacher with her friends from high school, Jess had naturally been all enthusiasm. Jess would have been all enthusiasm if Ava had told her that she wanted to be a rock star. But the others had expressed doubt or concern. One less-than-tactful girl had put it this way—if she was Ava's student, she would walk all over her. Those words had been ringing in her ears and heart ever since.

How could someone who she just met instill such confidence in her? His short statement steadied and refreshed her like nothing had for a long time, and even though she still doubted his faith in her success was completely warranted, it made her happy to believe that he could be right. Why couldn't she connect with older kids, or younger, or do anything that God wanted her to do, for that matter? She was willing and able to learn. She didn't know why such a simple concept—do your best and everything will turn out in the end—seemed so hard to hold on to sometimes.

She felt a twinge of guilt as she thought about her initial impressions of Pete. Tonight, he had been quick to offer her the guidance she desperately needed. But did he have to act so arrogant about it? She thought about the boldness in his expression when he caught her looking at him on Sunday, or his insinuation that she may not show up to their appointment on time. She supposed nothing that he had said or done since the time they met *really* could be labeled as arrogant versus simply being self-assured. Either quality was too liable to be a sin in her eyes, probably due to her own shyness.

Sure, she could have this moment of sensible introspection this evening, but one thing she was confident about was that the next time he smirked, teased, or boasted, she wouldn't be quite so able to hold on to her objectivity. Something about his manner made her blood pressure spike with irritation, and it made her feel more out of control than she was comfortable with.

# # #

Pete was beat by the end of the night and didn't have much time to think about Ava, between crashing into bed and working through the next day. But when he pulled into Jake's driveway Thursday night to watch the Eastern Conference Finals, his family was ready for him.

Pete had barely sat down when Jake said, "I noticed that you sat next to Ava at church last night."

"I sat next to Jon. And what kind of greeting is this? I thought you asked me over to watch basketball."

"Ava's so sweet," Amber commented, sweeping into the living room with Ivy on her hip. *So, they wanted to tag team him,* Pete thought. *Fine. He could take it.*

Jake continued, not at all discouraged by his noncommittal answers. "What did you guys talk about?"

"Getting her to the next step in her career," Pete grunted.

"Career advice!" Amber chirped. "Making yourself a shoulder to lean on, helping her gain some stability in the area... sounds like a great move to me."

"Look, don't read too much into this, okay? This isn't some kind of romance movie."

Amber clutched a hand to her heart. "That sounds exactly like something that the leading man in a romance movie would say!"

Pete sighed. "Just don't get your hopes up. I'm not planning anything and, like I said, I'm not interested." *Well, the first part was true.*

His sister-in-law patted his arm. "I know you aren't planning anything. That's why it's a good thing you have us."

Pete was saved when the three-year-old in Amber's arms stretched her chubby fingers in his direction. He took Ivy onto his lap and relaxed as he bounced her on one knee, sending her into a fit of shrieks and giggles. Rosalie, hearing the commotion and not wanting to be outdone, came running in soon after. She shot off a rapid-fire stream of questions, just as relentless—albeit more innocuous in subject matter —as her parents.

"What did you do today? Did you get anyone in trouble at school? Have you bought my birthday present yet?" On and on she went. Pete loved his nieces. He loved kids. It had always been a dream of his to have a family of his own, but he was waiting for just the right woman. He had been waiting for a decade and a half. At that thought a sickly feeling twisted in his stomach, but he stamped it out before it could settle there. He had already decided that being alone for the rest of his life was much better than settling down with someone that he couldn't rely on. And most people, he couldn't rely on.

He had a great job, a loving family and church, and the freedom to buy and do pretty much anything he wanted. A little loneliness was worth keeping the good things he had, if he could just get his head on straight. It's not like he needed a woman to be happy. He had built a stable life from the ground up with God's help alone, and that was the way it had to stay.

Pete was glad Amber and Jake seemed to be done needling him about his love life for the night. Drowning in a sea of emotions did not and would never fit his character description, no matter what Amber had said. He thanked his sister-in-law as she offered him a soda; then, his attention caught on Jake's 50-inch screen. As the home team burst into the court, Pete lost himself in the excitement of a high-stakes game enjoyed with good company.

5

Saturday, Ava sipped on her iced caramel macchiato while trying to preserve the lipstick she had applied for today's special occasion: the first day with customers. She blessedly was able to finish the cup before walking into Hydrangea, and told herself that while the caffeine and sugar kick wasn't the best long-term habit to be forming, the temporary buzz of energy and joy sparking in her veins would help her get off to the best possible start.

Though Ava had made it a point to come in several minutes early, Jenny was already doling out their work assignments for the day. When Ava joined the briefing, she received a winsome smile from Jackson. There was some definite heart pounding going on that had nothing to do with the drink she had just ingested.

Jenny turned her attention to Ava. "You'll start on this register and move to the floor after two hours," she told her.

"Yes, ma'am." Ava would look forward to the second rotation more, which would give her the flexibility to walk around and converse longer with individual customers. Mariana received the opposite assignment, and Ava squeezed her new friend's hand reassuringly. She could tell Mariana was all nerves and excitement. She hoped it would help that Mariana's assigned schedule built up the pace of her morning gradually.

The girls put their bags away and returned in time for Jenny's pep talk. Competence shone through their manager's poised demeanor, and her friendly words downplayed the gravity of the moment.

"Good morning to you all. We've assembled a great team here, and I know we are going to have a successful day. Not everything will go as planned, but we'll get through it as best we can, and as always, I am here to support you. Now, let's open this store!"

The associates clapped politely, most a little uncertain of the appropriateness of following a staff briefing with a loud whooping session.

Off they went, and although she was a seasoned sales veteran, Ava couldn't help inhaling a sharp intake of breath upon seeing the mass of people waiting outside for the doors to open. As they filtered in, she waited politely, answering questions and pointing folks in the right directions until the customers settled on what they wanted about a half-hour in. After that, she could barely catch her breath as a never-ending stream of mothers, daughters, and friends came forward with their purchases. By the time Mariana came to relieve her, Ava could hardly stop her hands from following the repetitive cycle of scanning, cashing, and wrapping.

A little before noon Ava was surprised to see three friendly faces appear: Amber, Rosalie, and Ivy Harrison. "Hey!" she exclaimed. "What are you guys doing here?"

"We came to see you on your first day of work!" Rosalie said, twisting the toe of her sneaker around in circles.

"That is so nice." Ava took stock of the two cotton sundresses draped across their mother's arm and held up a finger. "Wait here just a minute."

Expertly, Ava maneuvered through the racks to locate a pair of hair flowers—one a sunny yellow, and one plum-colored—and coordinating sparkly gladiator sandals. In Ivy's size, the shoes were of the jelly variety, which Ava always found to be the cutest. Sure enough, when the girls emerged from the dressing room, they were brimming with delight.

Ava clasped her hands together. "Oh, you both look so beautiful!" Ava turned to Amber and whispered, "My treat."

"Oh, no," Amber protested.

"Really, I insist. At least let me get the accessories. I get a great employee discount!" Amber nodded her head, and for the hundredth time, Ava thought to herself, *Best. job. ever.* If only she could make 40k with benefits selling jelly slippers for the rest of her life, she would be a happy woman.

After receiving a sweet trio of hugs, Ava steered the ladies to the checkout. Even though she found it difficult to catch on to the slew of new names and faces at Summer Shores Church, Ava was thankful that she could already feel such a close connection with these three members. After they left, the time flew until her lunch break. She was not a little excited to notice Jackson heading to the back room to punch out at the same time.

He turned her way. "What do you say I show you around town?"

Ava snorted. "You're new here too, and we only have thirty minutes."

Jackson amended, "Ok, what do you say I show you a coffee shop down the street?"

"Sounds good to me." Ava tried to sound casual, and also tried not to imagine what the effects on her already wired limbs would be after consuming *two* cups of coffee, compared to her usual daily total of zero. She thought, *is this a date?*

They stepped outside, and some looming storm clouds made the temperature feel bearable. Ava was thankful—she would just as soon not be a sweaty mess for their time together.

Hydrangea was a standalone building, but its street housed several other businesses which grew closer together the nearer they got to downtown. Ava grew quiet, alternating between taking note of a pet store, a pizzeria, and a doctor's office, and surreptitiously glancing at her tour guide. It was fair to say that she was dazzled by his good looks. She had casually dated her share of golden-hearted nerds, but never anyone so handsome and built.

Wanting to hold up her end of the conversation (and hoping she didn't sound too flirty), Ava asked, "Do you play any sports?"

"Lots, but mainly hockey."

"I'm sure that's a challenge down here!"

"I have to drive a while to get to the rink. I don't do it as often as I used to." He sighed and patted his stomach. "I'm getting way out of shape."

"Yeah, right!" Ava said, her eyes falling on his shirtsleeve, hugging one ripped bicep.

"I'm serious, come with me sometime and you'll see."

"No thanks. I'd be clinging to the wall as you skated circles around me. Dancing was my sport." Ava stabbed a finger at him in preemptive defense. "It is a sport!"

"Of course!" he said, eyes twinkling.

Jackson came to a stop before a cozy little building nestled up against a lakeside pier. She let out an involuntary sigh as a breeze rippled over the water. "It's perfect."

A bell tinkled over the door as they walked in. Ava was relieved to see a section of fruit smoothies chalked onto the coffee shop's menu and ignored the raised eyebrow Jackson shot her for wasting a trip to a great café on plain old strawberry banana. He paid, but she tried not to read too much into it, seeing as their orders totaled a whopping fifteen dollars. *He's probably just being an upstanding guy.* He motioned toward the back of the café, pulled out a stool for her, and bowed gallantly before sliding on his own. *He's definitely being an upstanding guy*, she thought.

He rested his chin on interlaced fingers. "Do you regularly visit coffee shops without getting coffee?"

"I admit, I can't handle it as well as some." Ava eyed his large double-shot expresso while unrolling her lunch bag. "But a smoothie goes better with turkey!"

"Mmh, I disagree," he said, unwrapping a large sandwich from the shop. "Coffee goes with everything. So, Miss Keller-Without-Coffee, tell me more about Ashwood."

Ava looked out at the water through the restaurant's tall windows. "I've lived there my whole life. My older sister got married and moved away. Then, my best friend from high school came down this way because of her husband's job. When I got the email about Hydrangea expanding into Florida, I applied for a transfer."

"What, couldn't find anyone else at home to run wild with?"

She laughed. "Wild isn't exactly the term I'd use. Jess and I used to go to the movies, to the nature center, to the roller rink...."

"Ok, sorry, I withheld judgement until I heard the words *roller rink*." Ava shoved Jackson playfully, and he relented, "Sorry. Please go on."

"Ashwood was a great place to grow up, actually. Not too fast-paced. There was room to breathe."

"Then why leave?"

Ava shrugged. "Talking about it now, it doesn't make much sense at all. But I guess I needed a change. Needed to see that I could make it in a new setting." She threw her arms out. "In paradise!"

"Makes perfect sense to me."

Flavor burst into Ava's mouth with her first sip of smoothie, and she decided that it was totally worth being victimized by coffee snobbery.

"So, what brought you here?" she asked.

"I got tired of arguing with my dad about the future," Jackson said, lifting his shoulder. "But as long as my hours are still pouring into his company, he doesn't care so much about where I do them."

"I'm sorry to hear that," Ava said, thinking about how her own mother called or texted her every day. She couldn't imagine a parent who didn't want to be around their child.

"It's not a big deal," Jackson replied.

Ava caught sight of the time on her phone. "We'd better start walking back."

His eyes held hers. "Already? We'll have to do this again sometime."

She gave him a small smile. "I'd like that."

Jackson threw out his garbage, having scarfed down his meal already. *He must need a lot of protein for all those muscles,* she thought idly, trying to stop herself from gawking again. As she sipped her smoothie side by side with him all the way back to the store, Ava couldn't help but feel that its taste was an apt metaphor for the way that she was feeling inside—perfectly sweet.

# # #

Jess assaulted Ava when she walked through the door. "How'd the first day go?"

For the one-hundredth time this week, Ava wondered how her friend could move so quickly with a twenty-pound infant on her hip.

"Let's talk sitting down, please!" Ava huffed. Trudging to the soft cream wraparound was a fatal mistake, she knew, as she kicked off her sturdy flats. There would be no getting up after this level of exhaustion. She answered, "Super busy. Buut—" She looked around, embarrassed at the thought of discussing the minutia of a nonexistent relationship in front of Isaac.

"Buut..." Jess prompted impatiently.

"I had lunch with Jackson."

Jess's bouncing had little to do with the baby on her knee, although Noah did seem to be appreciating her burst of energy. "Details!"

"He asked me to coffee." Jess nodded approvingly. "He paid," Ava continued, knowing that question was inevitable. "And we had a really nice time."

"Did he ask you out again?"

"It was hinted at. We exchanged numbers." Ava tried to shrug it off, but she couldn't help feeling a rush of pleasure. How exciting, that her lackluster love life might be getting an unexpected kickstart. *Maybe this place really is paradise,* she thought.

"Oh Ava, that's so great! And I know the perfect follow-up date! Let me just forward this to you." Jess tapped on her phone for a minute.

Ava's phone buzzed with an email from Amber Harrison, titled "Church Beach Day this Saturday!" complete with some cheery clip-art graphics. Jess said, "See, she even said specifically to invite you!"

"Super nice of her," Ava replied, biting her lip. "But I'm not sure I should be initiating beach dates after only five days of knowing someone."

"Already counting the days?" Jess teased.

Ava shook her head. "I should figure out if he is interested in church. I'm surprised that it hasn't come up yet. I guess I really don't know that much about him."

"Except that he's 'too perfect!'" Jess air-quoted Ava's exclamation from the other day.

"Okay, okay! I'm not scheduled to work next Saturday, so I'll come." As if there was any way to keep a landlocked, northern girl from the beach. "I'll text Jackson now too." *Before I lose my nerve.*

Ava: Hey! Some members of the church I've started going to are having a beach day on Saturday. If you're not busy, you're welcome to come with!

Jackson: Hey! I would love to, but I have to work, and I really need the hours.

Ava turned on Jess, who was reading the text over Ava's shoulder.

"See? Why did I let you talk me into this?"

Both girls shrieked in unison when they read the second text that came in.

Jackson: I am off Tuesday, however...

Ava: I get off at 4:30.

Jackson: It's a date.

6

Sunday morning was going well. This week at church, Ava knew where to turn to drop off Jess's dish, knew where to sit, and waved to the Harrison family, who was seated a few rows ahead of her. The Harrison family—who made her feel so welcome by coming to chat with her after service, walking her to the fellowship hall, taking her through the lunch line, and promptly filling in the chairs around Pete's table. Ava stopped and subtly scanned the room for Jess. *Still in line*, she noted. It would have been awkward not to sit with the Harrisons at that point, so she took the only remaining seat between Amber and Pete.

It wasn't so bad until the two little girls ran off to play after only a few bites of food, their mother chasing them down with their abandoned pizza slices in hand. Soon after, Jake shoveled in his last piece of key lime pie, picked up his plate and floated over to the pastor's table, muttering something about needing to make coffee.

Pete's face twitched, but he spoke after a moment of strained silence.

"So, did you leave a bunch of family in Iowa?" he asked. "They must be missing you pretty bad."

Her forehead creased. "Yeah, I miss them too. We're all really close. I have a sister who lives in Wisconsin." Her expression softened. "She has a baby on the way. I've always wanted to have a niece."

"When will the baby be here?"

"In about a month. They're going to call her Hope—isn't that beautiful? I'm already stocking up on cute clothes, and I have a list of books and movies we're going to watch together." She laughed. "I should probably give her a few years before I start all of that."

"Sounds like you're prepared."

"I've been waiting for this moment my whole life!"

"Is where your sister lives far from your hometown?"

"Only a few hours away. And only 21 hours from here," she said wryly.

"It's hard to be out on your own," Pete said. "I'm from Chicago, originally. I still go back and visit Mom and Dad from time to time. It's a good thing Jake followed me down here as soon as I left. He had enough of me bragging about the weather."

"There's not much to brag about now!"

He shrugged. "You get used to the heat. Just wait until January."

If I'm here that long. She was distracted from that disconcerting thought by Elizabeth Allen's appearance behind Pete. She was in a wheelchair, being pushed along by a young man who Ava figured must be her grandson.

Ava reached out a hand to lay overtop Elizabeth's fragile one. "I was so sorry to hear about your fall!" she said.

Elizabeth shook her head. "I can't believe I tripped on that step! I've gone up it a hundred times with no problems. I'll just have to be more careful next time." She smiled. "The Lord was still looking out for me. I was able to reach my phone. I called Pastor Thomas and he called Pete." Elizabeth extended her other hand to pat Pete's arm. "My family lives two hours south of here and couldn't drive up quick enough. Pete took me to the hospital and waited with me until they arrived."

"It was nothing," Pete said. "Anyone would have done the same thing if they lived in town."

"It wasn't nothing to me," she replied warmly. "Thank you again." Pete returned her smile.

Elizabeth sighed, looking from Pete to Ava. "It's nice to see two such fine young people here, getting along so well. Well, son, I guess you'd better take me home." Elizabeth squeezed Ava's hand, released it, and her grandson wheeled her away. As they left, Ava could swear that she heard Elizabeth whisper to Pete, "Don't mess this up."

Ava waved goodbye, confused. She turned back to Pete. "That was nice of you," she said.

"Not really. Josiah just called me because he knew I had nothing better to do."

"Still, you showed up. Elizabeth seems to think very highly of you."

"She's as nice as can be."

"Yep." After an awkward second, Ava figured that she and Pete had sat alone long enough and offered to take his silverware to the sink. He assented with a thanks and rose to go join his brother's table. Entering the kitchen, Ava found a tall woman at the sink and asked if she could help with anything.

"Aren't you the sweetest! Thank you! You can load those in the dishwasher if you want." The lady turned the water on and started handwashing the serving bowls. "It's Ava, right?"

"Yeah! How'd you know?"

"I'm Jon's mom. Joy Markham."

"Okay! He and I were talking the other day."

Joy's willowy frame and light brown hair were like her teenage son's, but her eyes were a warm chocolate color, in sharp contrast to Jon's vivid blue.

Ava stuck her and Pete's forks into the grate and was left empty-handed. "Do you want me to dry those for you?" she asked Joy.

"Sure. There's some clean towels in that drawer." Joy looked up to make sure Ava found what she needed, and continued rinsing. "I'm glad Jon's making more friends in the church. It's been a tough couple of years for us."

"Really?"

"My husband passed away from cancer," Joy's voice broke. "I'm sorry, it's still hard for me to talk about." She swallowed hard and put on a smile. "But God gives me grace every day." Seeing Ava frozen uncertainly with a toweled-off bowl, Joy pointed her in the direction of the cabinet that held the church dishes.

Grateful for the guidance, Ava held the cabinet door open for a moment. She didn't know what she should say. It felt too forward to hug a person she just met, and she knew that she couldn't pretend to imagine what Joy was going through.

"I'll keep you in my prayers," Ava said, meaning it. Her heart ached.

"Thank you, honey. I appreciate that."

Once the sink was cleared, Joy huffed out a breath. "I guess I'd better go wipe down those tables down." Grabbing a dishcloth, she added, "Thanks for listening."

"Of course." Ava stayed behind to finish drying the last few dishes, still thinking about how unsettling it must have been for Joy to lose her life partner. Apart from a few lines around her eyes, Ava never would have guessed that the woman had been through such a hardship. Ava felt like she couldn't handle the slightest disturbance in her own plans without falling to pieces.

Joy modeled a self-possession that Ava needed more of in her life. She wanted to be able to let go of her worries, to move forward and take on whatever challenge the day brought. Joy had gotten there—after all that she had been through, she was still standing—wiping away grime from dirty dishes, and whisking away nerves from a newcomer at church. Ava could only hope that, in time, she would get to that peace-filled place, too.

When she stacked the last plate in the cabinet, a text came through, reminding Ava that not all types of anticipation were bad. It was Jackson—he still wouldn't tell her where they were going for their date Tuesday. A smile played across her face as she texted him back with another guess, daydreaming about what would happen once they were together again.

# # #

A few minutes before six—the time that they had agreed to meet—Jackson finally texted Ava an address. She knew that the street was nearby but didn't want to take the chance of a wrong turn. When she plugged the address in her phone's GPS, it recognized the location as a roller rink. She laughed. *Really, Jackson?* She ran back inside to grab a pair of long socks, thankful that she had opted for jeans and a teal blouse, rather than for a skirt.

He was waiting for her in front of the entrance when she pulled in. His hands were in his pockets and he was watching her with that irresistible grin.

"Thought I'd make you feel at home," he said in explanation when she walked toward him.

"How kind of you."

They stepped inside; darkness and music surrounded them. It was a *cosmic* roller rink. Neon paint covered the walls to look like graffiti, and the man at the admission window handed Jackson a small packet of glow sticks.

"Fancy!" Ava said.

"Only the best for you," Jackson replied, splitting up the goodies. Their fingers brushed as she claimed her half, and a thrill ran through her.

"How do I look?" he puffed, modeling his new necklace and bracelet. His snug white shirt glowed purple under the black lights.

Incredible? Awe-inspiring? "It suits you," she said casually, snapping her own sticks as they walked to the skate rental counter.

He asked for inline skates, which was no less impressive than it was back when the boys used to whiz around in them in her fifth-grade skating parties. She stuck with the more stable, four-wheeled contraptions, hoping that she wouldn't look too awkward.

They laced up and he sprung gracefully to his feet. "Is there anything you aren't good at?" she asked miserably.

"I'm a terrible cook." He nodded to the concession stand. "It's pizza for you tonight!"

"As long as it comes with a freeze pop," she laughed. She thought that was smart of him to play to her sense of nostalgia for the first date. *As if he didn't have enough going for him!*

He helped her up and her hand tingled again. She wobbled slightly, and he said, "Do you want to practice over there?" He pointed to the only well-lit area in the rink, where a little kid was warming up with his mom. *Jerk.*

"No! I just need a minute to get steady on my feet." She pushed off a little too fast and thought, *a haughty spirit goes before a fall!*

Soon she was used to being in skates again. Jackson glided comfortably beside her until the music paused for a game of limbo. He looked to her with a challenge in his eyes and she nodded, skating into the line.

"I have to let you know, I was the limbo champion two years in a row when we came for school," she called to him. And she did make an impressive showing, making it to the final few rounds before the selfsame boy they had poked fun at earlier beat her out.

She returned to Jackson—whose massive frame made him an early elimination—and shrugged her shoulders. "I guess I don't have what it takes anymore."

"You made it far," he offered.

"At least I figured out there's two things you're not good at!"

"I'll rely on you to keep me humble," he said as they returned to skating laps.

The limbo competition was topped by a game she had never played: "Who Can Sing the Loudest?"

She and Jackson sang their hearts out, barely breathing between shrieks of laughter. Naturally, the most powerful belter in the room was...the little boy. As he rolled over to collect his candy prize, Ava said to console herself, "He's going to have a hard time going to bed tonight after all that sugar."

The culmination of the evening's enjoyments was a couple's skate—the horror of every single person and the anticipation of every newly dating one.

Jackson interlocked his large fingers with hers and she felt dizzy. *Pull yourself together, Ava, for goodness' sake.*

She knew that she had a penchant for over-romanticizing events in her head, thinking the best of people to a fault. It had burned her in the past, but Jackson hadn't been anything but a perfect gentleman. *Be careful, you don't know him very well,* a little voice in her head said, which she promptly squelched down. She was always being so negative. Maybe Jess was right, and she should expect something good for a change.

When the slow song ended, Jackson asked, "Do you want to get something to eat?"

"Sure," she squawked, then cleared her throat. He kept hold of her hand as they skated over to the tables, and he ordered them each a huge slice of cheese pizza and a pop.

As she sat down on a plastic chair, the adrenaline left her. *I'm going to be sore tomorrow,* she thought. She made a mental note to set aside time to start working out.

"I'm glad I brought the roller-skating queen of Ashwood back to her first love," Jackson said, handing her a can.

"You definitely have. I'm going to resent you for this because, before, I didn't remember what I was missing. Now I'm going to have to come back here all the time."

"I'm glad. I was worried when I saw the light of limbo-glory leave your eyes."

"I am a grown woman." Ava sniffed. "I do not need a prize to validate my importance."

"We could always come after the kid's bedtime," he countered.

"Deal."

Ava couldn't believe that she had made it twenty-three years in Iowa without any lasting prospects, and now, a week into her extended vacation, someone like Jackson was hinting at a second date. Someone from Iowa, no less! They had so much in common—they could travel back and see their families together...she didn't want to get too far ahead of herself, but she thought, *God could really be working in this.*

"Listen, I have a favor to ask." Jackson's eyebrows raised in earnest, but then he lowered his head, shaking it. "No, forget it. I know you're busy."

"What is it?" Ava scooted closer.

He looked up at her and her eyes caught in his seafoam ones. She found herself idly wondering how not a single, gelled-back dark hair on his head ever looked out of place.

"It's just that, I finished the application that they make you fill out when you want to volunteer overseas. I had to write this essay about how my 'life journey' led me to want to serve. I know it's no good. I thought maybe since you are going to be an English teacher, you could look over it for me."

"Yeah, no problem. I'd love to."

His lips parted in surprise. "Really?"

"Really. Give me your phone and I'll put in my email."

"You're the best."

Ava replied with a nonchalant "hmm," while she typed, as if Jackson's words of praise didn't make her insides soar.

Though her insides may have been soaring, her outside was bloated and fatigued by their juvenile fare. Jackson claimed the same, so the pair opted to call it a night. Back on the rink's hard plastic benches, Ava ditched her socks and slipped into her flats, wiggling her numbing toes. Jackson, who didn't have long laces to unknot, finished first and returned their skates.

The couple meandered outside, and the charged moment of the end of a first date was upon them. He turned to her but spared her any internal warring by planting a soft kiss on her cheek. He gave her a swift hug and looked into her eyes. "I had a great time tonight."

"Me too." She would cherish every moment.

"I'll see you at work." He let go of her shoulders reluctantly, and she headed back to Isaac's car. Ava drove home in a daze, trying not to let a thousand visions of the future dance in her head. She let herself in using the spare key that the Wilsons had given her. Jess was in the nursery with Noah, so Ava walked quietly to her room, took off her glow sticks, and arranged them in a place of honor upon her bedside table.

7

Ava pulled Jackson's essay up on her computer as soon as she got an email from him the morning after their date. She wanted him to know that he hadn't thought wrong when he decided to rely on her for help.

She had become so used to putting Jackson on a high pedestal that she was surprised to see so many colorful underlines scattered across the document—misspellings, duplicated words, inconsistent capitalization and punctuation. Nevertheless, his charming voice still shone through from the very first line. She trudged through every word until she had shaped the essay into something readable:

I'm not going to lie, I was intimidated when I read that I had to have a "life journey" in order to apply for your program. See, the truth is that my life journey has been pretty easy so far. I've lived a life of privilege, getting anything I've ever wanted. Sounds great, except that I've never really felt like I've done something that mattered.

When I got to high school, they made me take one of those surveys that told you where you should go when you graduate. My personality lined up well with careers involving travel, which sounded perfect to me. Your program showed up under my results, and, clicking through your website, I found some pictures of Costa Rica.

Apply for a job where you can play soccer and ride around on four-wheelers for a year? Escape into the jungle, see trees and mountains so tall that they defy comprehension? Sleep on hammocks, next to pools of calm water, and just forget all the problems that we rich kids come up with? I could think of no greater adventure. Please consider me for your program. You will find no happier candidate than in me.

After attaching her revisions, Ava added to her reply email:

My only suggestion would be to talk more about not only why you need the trip, but also how you will make a difference for them. More along the lines of what you were mentioning the first day that we met. I think that you are going to knock it out of the park!

Jackson replied right away: **You are beyond incredible! How can I ever thank you?**

Ava: Promise me that you'll never buy me pizza, grande nachos, or gummy worms again.

Jackson: Fair enough. Human bodies are not meant to consume that much sugar and sodium at one time.

Ava: Oh, to be young again and eat whatever we want.

Ava loved the fluttery feeling that talking to Jackson gave her. And, after reading his essay, Ava knew with even greater conviction that they had so much in common. Ava's parents cared for her deeply, unlike what Jackson's situation sounded like with his dad, but she knew what it was like to want to prove herself. And to not quite feel like she belonged.

Maybe his move down to Florida wasn't a big enough change for Jackson to feel like he could make it on his own. Ava could relate to his feeling of wanting to move on from a longtime job into something more permanent and meaningful—a calling.

Here she was in June already, and Ava was no closer to discovering hers. But she had to remind herself of the observation appointment coming up with Pete, where at least she could gain some more information about what it would really be like to work in a school.

Plus, she had that trip to the ocean coming up. It was hard for her to let go and truly enjoy her free time without feeling like she should be getting everything sorted out, but she was working on it. She was doing what she could, and taking steps to reach her goals. She couldn't force her future into being. And, if she kept spinning her wheels, she would only wear herself out.

# # #

Beach day. Pete glanced at the rolled-up towel and dirty baseball cap on his leather passenger seat and asked himself again *why* had he shown up to beach day? Carpooling was out of the question—as appealing an idea as it was to squeeze in the back of Amber's SUV between two squirming nieces. Of course, he pulled in at the exact same time as Isaac's crew. Ava sprang out of the side door, not looking the least bit annoyed at sharing a row with her friend's kid. She even stuck her head back into the van to entertain Noah as his mom pulled out bags and bags of supplies.

Ava's swim cover was classy and covering but showed off her delicate arms and shoulders. Pete was never a fan of oversized ponchos, or those tassel things on the bottom that looked like they should be on a curtain instead of women's clothing, but somehow, she made it work. He was all at once glad and kicking himself that he came. *Too late to change your mind now.* He called out, "Hey, you guys need some help with those?"

Jess beamed "No!" at the same time her husband shouted, "Yes!" and the men exchanged grins. Pete walked over to relieve Isaac's shoulder of one of its striped umbrellas.

"You come well-prepared," Pete huffed as he scooped up an oversized duffel.

"We have to show Ava a good time today!" Jess nodded cheerily to her friend. "We've picked up a few necessities in a year. And babies come with a lot of stuff, anyway."

Pete turned his gaze to Ava, who smiled shyly back. He asked, "We're still on for your observation Wednesday, right? You didn't forget?"

Her smile puckered so quickly that he almost laughed. "Of course I didn't!" she said.

"Good. The kids are excited for you to come."

"I can't say that I'll be that exciting, but I'm looking forward to it too."

"Nothing to worry about, they're just second-graders. They don't bite..." *Too bad,* he amended, recalling one student who had ended his seatmate's teasing with his teeth. That was one of his stranger days at work.

They walked from the parking lot over grass-spotted sand dunes until they came within view of the shore. Though Pete wasn't usually the sentimental type, he wasn't immune to the sea's churning power. It was hard in a place like this not to feel God's presence and remember that He is ultimately in control. The scene seemed to have an even bigger impact on Ava. Her hands slackened on her bag and her lips parted. She turned her head slowly from one side to the other to take in the sea, and then lifted her eyes to the sky.

Pete could relate. Coming to Florida for the first time, it was like, *Man, I live here.* Sometimes it still felt like a dream, and he was glad about that. He wanted to always remember all that he'd been given.

"Uncle Pete, Uncle Pete!" Rose and Ivy's shrieks cut through the wind from somewhere downhill, and they soon ran up to meet him.

"No, no, no!" He just managed to shrug off his burden before they leapt into his arms and started crawling onto his back. Though the pair were usually angels in public, they could really get wound up when they got excited.

"Come and swim with me," Ivy started tugging on Pete's arm.

"Hold on, you little maniacs!" Pete put them down and moved the Wilsons' stuff next to his sunbathing sister-in-law. He waved to Amber in greeting, then dutifully followed the girls to where they had abandoned their dad, who was hard at work on an epic sandcastle.

"Aren't you a little old to still be playing in the sand?" Pete asked him.

Jake put his shovel down to assess his brother, and then to take in the other new arrivals. "Peter. I'm surprised to see you here. Don't you always say that the beach is too messy and too far away for you to waste a Saturday on? I wonder why you decided to come *this* time..."

"Yeah, Uncle Pete, why did you decide to come *this* time?" Rosalie echoed.

Pete shot Jake a warning look so that he wouldn't wrap the innocent girl up in his scheming, and lifted Rose up and over his shoulder. "I came to get my nieces soaked!" Holding her tight and

49

feeling her tiny fists beating down on his back in a combination of delight and fury, Pete ran into the waves.

# # #

Ava's eyes trailed Pete and Rosalie, and she mused about how sweet it was that the girls loved their uncle so much.

"Hi, I'm so glad you all could come!" Amber called.

"Thanks so much for inviting me," Ava replied, taking in the row of other church members' families scattered down the beach on wide, slick blankets. She waved to Joy Markham—the woman who had helped her in the kitchen last Sunday—and shot Jess a look of fresh appreciation at all the gear she had made them tow. Ava would be enjoying the beach like a native Floridian now.

Amber patted the spot next to her and leaned into the sun, enjoying the moment of peace. Ava sat down, and Amber peered at her through wide sunglasses.

"You did put on sunscreen, right?"

"Oh yeah, I covered up on the way here." Ava wrinkled her nose, the chemical smell still potent on her skin. "I don't usually burn though. I might pink up a little on my cheeks."

"Lucky," Amber sighed with a glance at her own fair arms. "But I'll have to warn you, the sun is strong here!"

"Noah and I are going to collect seashells," Jess interjected, a bright red bucket hanging from one finger. "Want to come with?"

"No thanks, I'll be all right here," Ava answered. Jess turned back hurriedly to keep her little tike from eating sand.

Amber looked over with joy at her own family splashing in the shallows. "So," she said lightly. "Have you had a chance to get to know my brother-in-law, Pete?"

"A little," Ava shrugged. "He seems like a nice guy," she added, wanting to keep things positive, Amber being his family member and all.

"Nice enough to go on a date with?" Amber asked with a hopeful smile. Ava's jaw dropped. *Ok, the floodgates are open now!*

"Umm… I don't really think he's my type." Amber was prying bigtime. Ava knew it came from a good place—she was trying to throw in a good word for her family—but everyone's continual need to throw her together with men was really getting old.

Amber persisted, "What is your type? If you don't mind me asking."

Ava sighed. "Someone who always thinks about how other people feel before they speak. Someone ambitious. A little charity work wouldn't hurt." Ava decided that was a sufficient portrait of her knight in shining armor.

"That does sound great!" Amber paused. "You know, though, people can surprise you."

"People don't change," Ava shot back. *Goodness, Ava, bitter much?*

Amber inclined her head in acquiescence. "No, they don't change easily. And certainly not without God's help." She pursed her lips. "My advice, my unsolicited advice, would be to make sure that you have the *right* things in common."

Ava turned her gaze to Amber's husband, swinging Ivy back and forth in his arms. At least Amber was laying off on the Pete subject. Ava acknowledged, "I should always be grateful for wisdom, solicited or not. It looks like things worked out perfectly for you."

Amber shone with pure contentment. "Yes. I'm blessed with so much more than I ever could've imagined for myself. It hasn't been perfect—we're not perfect people. Still, I've been so, so happy." She turned a compassionate eye towards Ava. "I remember what it was like, you know. Watching and waiting for the right guy to come along. Don't lose hope."

Ava's eyes stung at hearing her oft-felt disappointment vocalized. "Thanks. I know it's so cliché, but I'm scared of opening myself up and getting hurt again."

"Make a list," Amber suggested, "of things that are really important to you. And maybe leave out the charitable work," she winked. "I mean real non-negotiables. Also, enjoy the special time you have with God now. The more you are grounded in His truth, the better wife you will be when you do meet 'the one.'"

"You mean IF," Ava corrected.

"WHEN," Amber smiled. Ava wasn't so confident as to be assured of that, but if Jess's joy could shoot through Ava like a bolt of lightning, the words of her newfound friend soaked into her bones like a gentle rain. It wasn't that Ava *wanted* to be faithless in God, or unsatisfied at being alone. She simply couldn't imagine feeling any other way.

She mentally recited Matthew 6:34, as she often had to do to stay anchored: "Take therefore no thought for the morrow: for the morrow

51

shall take thought for the things of itself." Not easy for a compulsive over-planner, but it did put some breath back in her lungs.

"Thanks. Maybe I will try making a list," Ava said. "It does help me to put my thoughts down on paper. Unless it's a to-do list—that just stresses me out!"

Amber scoffed, "To-do lists. I put something on there and then never look at it again. If I keep forgetting to do my to-do's, then they must not be *that* important, right?"

"Definitely," Ava laughed, "especially for someone as busy as you."

"Come on, let's go cool off." Amber tossed her head in the direction of the water, much to Ava's relief. She could feel her skin scorching after only a few short minutes of conversation.

Jess, Noah, and the Jake Harrison family were close enough to the ocean for their toes to be lapped with foam, but the other men had ventured out deeper to jump waves. Jess waved Ava on, not needing assistance with the three little ones now that Amber was joining them.

Ava waded out to Isaac and Pete's bobbing figures, and Isaac kindly tried to teach her the proper technique. She bounced on her tiptoes facing the incoming wave, her muscles taut, but still ended up bowled over, choking down a slap of saltwater. *Nothing more attractive than snot and tears running down your sputtering face*, Ava thought, mortified.

After a few more beatings, Ava decided to crawl back up the sand, being painfully reminded—once again—that she needed to get back in the habit of working out. She went to play with the toddlers where it was safe. A while later, she felt the skin of her back start to tighten incrementally. Her eyes widened.

"There's no way my sunscreen wore off already!" She looked to Jess for reassurance, who shook her head vigorously and threw her a bottle of lotion.

"Reapply, reapply!"

She slathered the goop on extra thick, as if that could somehow compensate for her forgetting. When she leaned over to return the sunscreen to Jess's beach bag, her heart jumped, seeing a missed call from Jackson on her cell. Wiping her hand off on a towel, she grabbed the phone and scrambled to her feet, nearly bumping into Pete and Isaac who were coming to dry off. "I have to take this," she said, looking at Jess significantly.

"Go!" her friend pointed her in the direction of a wooden pavilion.

Ava hurried up the shoreline and called. Jackson picked up right away.

"Hey," she said.

"Hey, you."

"Aren't you at work?" she asked, double-checking the time.

"I'm on break," he answered.

"Oh. Well, thanks for spending it on me!"

"Anytime."

"I'm sorry you couldn't come today, but this guy from church, Jon, invited everyone to his house Friday night for a barbeque. It sounds kind of fun. Would you want to go?" She held her breath as she waited for him to respond.

"Oh." He sounded disappointed. "I'd love to, but I promised my buddy I'd help him move that day."

"On a Friday?" she asked.

"Yeah, he's off...he's got a crazy work schedule like us."

"Okay," she said with mock cheer, her heart sinking. She hoped it really was a case of bad timing and that he wasn't trying to make up excuses so he didn't have to hang out with church people. She didn't want to be pushy, but would have to feel the issue out soon.

"See you Monday?" she asked. That was the next time they would be working together.

"Wouldn't miss it!" She could almost see his smirk through the phone.

"Yeah, you wouldn't miss it—you'd get a write-up," she laughed. "But I appreciate the thought."

"Until then, beautiful," he said. Her pulse raced.

"Bye."

Ava walked back to her party, breathless. She grinned at Jess, who gave her a knowing look. Pete turned his back on her altogether. *What was that all about?* she wondered.

She shrugged off his strange behavior. Nothing could ruin this day.

Even the peeling, itching, and angry redness that her skin suffered for days afterward didn't seem so bad (although that may have been because Jess succored her with a healthy dose of aloe vera in true mom-like fashion). Jackson thought she was beautiful, she was making new friends, and she was surrounded by sunshine and incredible experiences.

8

On the long drive home from the beach, Pete remembered Isabelle. He thought, *Since Ava already messed with my head today, I might as well.* The last time he went to the coast was with his ex-girlfriend. He spent the trip rejoicing in the way her long, dark hair snapped in the breeze, how good her tan, athletic figure looked with the horizon as a backdrop, and how unbelievable it was that she had chosen him.

In retrospect, he could see that that had been what Isabelle was thinking too—*Pete's so lucky that a girl like me would give him the time of day.* Though she easily danced alongside the shore in a bikini, or smirked at men's awestruck stares in a restaurant, Pete knew that deep down she must have some longstanding insecurity. Why else would she constantly needle him to tell her how amazing she was, or put down everyone that she met? It must have given her some sense of power to have a man who would drop any obligation or drive any distance to help her with a problem, because she made him do that all the time.

And what did he get for bending over backwards? She showed up at his apartment unannounced one night—but that wasn't anything new—sat on his couch, started scrolling through her phone, and sighed like the trip had put her out. "I'm moving to California," she stated simply.

"What?"

She looked at him as if he were an idiot and spoke more slowly. "I'm moving to California."

"Why?"

55

"I just don't belong here anymore. Acting, modeling, that's where my future is. Not," she flicked her fingers disdainfully, "here."

"Alright." Pete said. He didn't entirely blame her for the way she started stretching out every syllable—he *was* having a hard time following the conversation. "So we'll do long distance."

She turned to face him fully then, and his stomach turned to lead. "This isn't working out," she said. "I know you're feeling it too."

He wasn't. How was he supposed to see this coming when she had strolled in two minutes earlier and taken a handful of his Cheetos?

The rest of the scene he didn't care to relive. He went from anger, to denial, to—shamefully—pleading, but she had made up her mind.

Logically, he knew how that train wreck happened—he was attracted to a shallow girl who sent his misgivings running with every bat of her eyelids. Now it seemed that his heart was dying for more self-destruction.

Sure, the two women couldn't be more different. Ava radiated sincerity—her emotions flashed across her face like an open book. She didn't vie for anyone's attention, yet was attentive to others—talking points that his family and even Pastor Thomas kept hassling him about. Pete shook his head at the memory. *What is the world coming to when a man can't rely on his own pastor to back him up?*

If they were honestly wanting to do him a favor, they would get off his back about it. From what he heard, Ava had moved to Florida for work, on a whim. She wouldn't stick around long. Already today, she was running off from her friends to enjoy the attention of some guy. And the last thing Pete wanted was to feel the way Isabelle had made him feel, *ever* again.

# # #

At work Monday afternoon, Ava was folding jeans into pristine stacks when she was startled by a low whine. As she approached the sound's source, the whine grew into a wail and she discovered a family of three down a crowded aisle of discount tops. Sweeping her eyes over the scene, she noticed that Jackson had come over to investigate too. She didn't want to make the family uncomfortable by offering unwanted assistance, but she pushed forward at the sight of the mother's thinly veiled panic.

"Excuse me," she called, clearing a path through the shoppers who hadn't already taken a hint and drifted away. "Can I help you?"

"I'm sorry," the mother said. "My daughter likes this shirt, but we can't find her size." She rubbed the back of a girl who was maybe eleven; the girl leaned over, clutching the ends of her long hair. The overwhelmed expression on her face broke Ava's heart.

She was instantly reminded of Jess's brother back home, who she had loved getting to know. Ben's disability came with sensory issues which made going out in public a challenge at times. Ava looked with fresh eyes at a dozen other customers chatting, the hangers in their hands screeching against the rack's metal rods, and the limited space in the row.

"Please, don't apologize," Ava said, with the kindest smile she possessed. She turned to address the daughter but kept a respectful distance. "Hi, I'm Ava. What's your name?"

"Riya," her mother answered for her.

"Riya, I'm going to our stockroom to look for some shirts." She looked from Riya's torso—which was slim, but longer than many of their younger customers'—to the offending fuchsia blouses in front of her. "Do you need a large?"

"Yes," Riya's mother replied. "That would be wonderful. Thank you so much."

"Of course," Ava said, already heading for the back. "I'll put together a few different choices and find you something really great!" On her way she caught Jackson's gaze and tilted her head slightly, telling him to take care of them while she was gone.

She had noticed Riya's brother, a teenager wearing a superhero shirt, lurking in the background, and hoped that Jackson could strike up a nice conversation with him. As surprising a hobby as it was for the Homecoming King, it seemed that he had an extensive knowledge of comic books, and they were already chatting as she walked away.

The racks in the steel-gray stockroom were meticulously organized, so it didn't take long for her to return with a couple different sizes of the coveted blouse (*thank the Lord there were still some left!*) as well as some similar jewel-hued options. Riya's joy was contagious as she took in the shirts draped across Ava's arm.

"Would you like to try these on?" Ava asked, and Riya's eyes sparkled in reply. She got the ladies set up in a spacious room and waited nearby, noting with pleasure that Jackson and the brother seemed to be hitting it off; they had barely noticed that the rest of their party had moved along.

To Ava's delight, Riya came out and modeled each new selection for her—the fuchsia scoop-neck set off her complexion beautifully. She looked sweet in a sapphire peasant top, and stunning in a golden tee studded with gems. Ava and Mom—who had introduced herself as Mrs. Patel—cheered and exclaimed until Riya was near bursting with pride. She laughed all the way to the checkout.

After making their purchases, Riya's mother returned to pull Ava in for a quick hug. Tears pricked in the back of Ava's eyes.

"Thank you," the woman whispered.

Ava shook her head. The family had blessed her today and not the other way around. "It was so nice to meet all of you. Please come again!"

"We will," Mrs. Patel called with a wave. Jackson reappeared at Ava's side and together, they watched the family exit the store. Jackson turned to her, eyebrows raised.

"You're amazing, you know that, right?"

Heat rushed to Ava's cheeks at the compliment, though she felt a twinge of guilt in her belly. She had just been doing her job as an employee and as a Christian—to do everything in her power to brighten the day of a person that she came across. It was a special pleasure to do that for a girl as sweet as Riya. She pushed her discomfort away in irritation. *Here the guy I am falling harder for than anyone I've ever met is calling me amazing, and I am going to complain about it?*

She settled on a simple "thanks," forcing herself to look him in the eye. He was staring back with unadulterated admiration. Suddenly worried that she would flush even deeper, Ava got back to work in a hurry. Yet she couldn't contain the smile that kept tugging at the corners of her lips for the rest of the day.

Stay cool, she chided, while altogether knowing that if she ever had a type, Jackson Green was it. With every new day that passed, she was in greater danger of falling in love with him.

# # #

That night, a video call came in from her sister.

Ava answered, "Hey! I've been thinking about you."

Julianne's fine, shoulder length hair was dyed a chestnut brown this month. It fell around the sides of her face as she leaned towards her phone, as if to get a better look at Ava. "I've been thinking about you too. How's Florida?"

"Fine," Ava brushed her question off. "How's the baby?"

"Wonderful," Julianne said, shifting the camera down for a belly shot.

"Oh my goodness!" Julianne had always been so tiny, but eight months of pregnancy had done its work. Her stomach was stretched into the compact shape of a basketball. "Hey there, baby," Ava said softly.

Julianne leaned back to rest against the carved headboard of her bed, folding one arm over her belly. "She is moving around all the time now."

"That doesn't sound comfortable."

"No, it isn't. I am sitting down a lot during the day. It's cool, though. This pregnancy thing is starting to feel more real— there is definitely someone inside of here waiting to come out."

Ava grimaced at that visual. "Are you taking your prenatal vitamins?" she asked.

"Yes, Mom, I am taking my prenatals. Honestly, you are full of so much research, a person would think that you're the one having this baby!"

"Believe me, I am well aware that I am a thousand years behind you in the family-building department. But I did take those parenting classes in high school. I just want to be..."

"Prepared," Julianne finished Ava's sentence with a laugh. "What am I going to do without my wise little sister?"

Although Juli's comment was light-hearted, guilt flared up in Ava's chest. There would be no more weekend trips to visit her sister, no late-night chats on the couch if she stayed in Florida. No movie days with homemade popcorn and hot chocolate. Once Hope was born, there would be no babysitting, or outings with Auntie. She asked herself, *Am I really prepared to be just a face that my niece sees when we talk on the phone?*

Julianne's face grew serious. "Ava, are you thinking too much again? How are things?"

"I'm missing you guys."

"I was just messing with you before. I'm happy for you. We will do better about staying in touch, from now on, I promise." She grinned conspiratorially. "You must not be having too bad of a time down there. Mom told me about Jackson."

Ava rolled her eyes, "Of course she did."

"So..." Juli drummed her fingers expectantly.

"Well, he's attractive and funny. But more than that, he is completely into me. He called me amazing today."

"Then he's smart, too."

"He's smooth... he's serious so infrequently that I can't get a great read on how smart he is. But he's driven." *And he's serious when he talks about how much he cares about me*, Ava thought, not sure if she wanted to share that part yet. Julianne sounded excited enough as it was.

"That's good."

Ava continued, "We both care about helping other people. Like, I was working with this wonderful customer at work today, and Jackson appreciated what I did so much. And, he's spontaneous. He took me for a roller rink for our last date. I can't wait to see what he has planned next."

"That is so great," Julianne was beaming.

"I don't think I've felt this way before about anyone," Ava admitted, playing with the edge of her bedsheet. "To have someone who seems to be all-in... it's what I've been looking for. He tells me that I'm beautiful, and calls all the time. I didn't know that relationships could be like this."

"Relationships? He's your boyfriend then?"

Hmm...is he? Ava thought. "Not in so many words. And I am not ready to bring up that conversation yet. I don't want to scare him off."

"Good guys don't get scared off. But I don't want to make you worry. Just, promise me that you'll be smart about this?"

"Okay," Ava said, with all the longsuffering of a younger sister used to being told what to do. It was true that Ava was usually the sensible one, but Juli was protective when she needed to be. That's how Ava knew that her sister was going to make a great mom.

Ava sighed, looking at the time. "I'd better go. They scheduled me to work early tomorrow."

"I forget that it's an hour later there."

"And you need plenty of rest, too," Ava said sternly.

"Yes, I do," Julianne acknowledged, sliding her head onto her downy pillow. "Goodnight, my love."

"Goodnight. Have a great week. And take care of that baby!" Ava had to add with a smile. Julianne nodded, and her comforting face blinked off of the screen the second she hit "end call." Just as immediately, Ava was overcome with loneliness.

But her phone buzzed with a text from Jackson, and she wasn't lonely anymore. She grinned, sinking lower into her bed, ready to get lost in another long conversation.

9

Wednesday morning, Ava slid her fingers over her face in an attempt to block out the sunlight streaming through the curtains. With a sigh, she blearily patted the top of the dresser until she hit her phone, and slid it close. The time read 9:30 over a notification—two missed calls from Pete Harrison. She shot up. *No, no, no!* No time for a shower, no time to stress about her outfit, and no way she was going to be less than two hours late to her appointment at Pete's school.

Thank goodness her wardrobe was already chock-full of dressy-casual. In the midst of colder weather, Ava and her mom had raided their mall's summer clearance racks for capris, polyester tanks, and sandals, knowing that Ava would soon be coming down to Florida.

She threw on a red-checkered dress, brushed, mascara-ed, and flew. When she got in the car, she dialed Pete on speakerphone while her GPS barked out orders, but he didn't pick up. She supposed it was admirable that he wasn't abandoning his classful of eight-year-olds to chat with one very tardy student observer.

She didn't know how she had managed to sleep through her compulsively-set double alarm system, but it may have had something to do with her late night texting Jackson.

Forty-five agonizing minutes later, Ava pulled into the parking lot at Citrus Grove Elementary. She let out a low whistle. It was still strange to her the way that schools down here, even the smaller ones, were set up like college campuses. A shady overhang connected rows of square buildings with a few common areas in between.

She almost lost a ballet flat on her way to the office, which was painted in a clean white with a splash of yellow behind the school's name. Before entering, she smiled and leveled out her breathing, figuring it wouldn't do to have an asthma attack on their front steps. Inside, she was greeted by a woman in her fifties with straight, salt-and-pepper hair.

"Welcome to Citrus Grove. How may I help you?" The secretary's smile was genuine and just what Ava needed to still her fidgeting.

"Hi, my name is Ava Keller. I was supposed to be in Mr. Harrison's class today?"

"Oh! Ms. Keller." The woman produced a sign-in sheet from a desk drawer. "Mr. Harrison was here this morning looking for you—I told him I'd keep an eye out."

"Yeah, I'm sorry I'm late!"

"No problem at all. He's going to be in the first building on your left when you exit."

"Thank you so much." The woman nodded, and Ava was on her way.

The room was clearly marked "Mr. Harrison's Second-Grade Class" on a laminated flyer of an orange tree. She was peering through the door's small window—hoping to remain inconspicuous—when she saw Pete, seated in a student chair in the center of a semi-circle of second graders, who were all shouting and pointing in her direction.

She sighed and pushed on the handle. "Guys," Pete announced, "say hello to Ms. Keller."

They did so with gusto; one boy even shouted, "Finally! We've been waiting for you forever."

"All right, that's enough. Get back to work," Pete said, and motioned for her to sit at his teacher's desk.

"I'm so sorry," she mouthed on the way over, and he shrugged. *I never do this, I swear!* her expression pleaded. Pete rose to look over a few students' notebooks, and Ava noticed the way the kids lit up when he came near. Honestly, it wasn't that different from what she had observed at church—it seemed with people, big or small, he didn't mind cracking a joke or calling someone out. And they loved it.

She was startled from her musings by a tiny voice saying, "You're pretty."

The voice belonged to a girl with brightly colored barrettes which clicked into each other at the end of every braid. Her nameplate read "Layla."

"Thank you, I think you're pretty too!"

The boy next to her asked Ava, "Are you Mr. Harrison's girlfriend? He doesn't have one yet, and he's getting really old!" Ava choked down some unprofessional laughter and schooled her features.

"No, I'm just a friend. I need to learn all about teaching, and Mr. Harrison said it would be okay if I hung out with you guys today, to see what your class is like."

"Mr. Harrison's the best, even though he talks too much. You can learn a lot from us."

"*You* talk too much, Gabe!" Layla turned back to Ava. "We're a little crazy sometimes, but we hope you like it here. You can stay as long as you want."

"That is so nice of you! I know I'm going to learn a lot today! Well, I'd better let you get back to work. Do you need help with anything?"

Layla picked up a pencil with a feathered end. "No, we're just writing a paragraph about what we're going to do this summer. You'd better sit down, your bag looks reeally heavy."

These kids were a riot. Ava felt instantly at ease and took Layla's advice. Seated, she pulled out her journal to jot down some notes about the classroom's organization, the schedule posted on the wall, and the colorful posters on everything from geography to prefixes.

"Hey," Pete approached, evidently content with the class's progress for the moment. "What are you doing?"

"Taking notes." He smirked at her, and she smiled back sheepishly. "I came with a few questions, too."

"Fire away."

"What has been your biggest challenge so far, and how did you face it?" she read.

Pete sat down and ran his fingers through his hair. "I feel like I'm at an interview!"

"Sorry!"

He brushed that off. "It's okay. It's good you want to learn so much. Um... I would say the biggest challenge of teaching is also the biggest reward. It is a lot to manage a class by yourself—Robert, knock it off!

—but at the end of the day, you just have to show them you care. If they know that, they'll listen to anything you've got to say."

"Wow," Ava said, awestruck for a moment before taking it down verbatim like a court reporter. "How long have you been teaching?"

"Four years."

"You teach all the subjects throughout the day? I'm not sure that I would like that."

"It's easy enough. You just go through the book, adding commentary, answering questions. Making sure they're understanding. The other second grade teachers helped me a lot when I first got started."

"That's good to know. I feel like all the college theories in the world aren't going to help me when I get in front of the kids alone." Ava shuddered at the thought.

"You have to go in with the expectation that your first year is survival," Pete said. "It gets easier with time. Even experienced teachers have tough days, but we all do the best we can."

Ava considered messing up in front of twenty-five children. Or worse, one hundred high-schoolers in the space of a day! She loved to feel in control, to take the time and practice enough to have mastery of any situation before performing a task. But she knew that God was nudging her in this direction. It would be selfish of her to let the fear of wounded pride get in the way of helping others. If someone who was as clearly gifted as Pete could have bad days, maybe Ava wouldn't mess up as badly as she imagined.

# # #

There she sat all day, scribbling notes in that ridiculous notebook, the picture of curiosity and attention. What struck Pete as so odd about Ava was that she was always content to listen. Most people (himself included) couldn't wait to get their opinions out, but she sat back, always pleasantly, taking everything in. Before now, he hadn't paid much attention to people who had nothing to say, but he couldn't seem to take his eyes off of Ava. There was a sharpness, an intelligence there that made him look forward to the next time she would speak. *Was she thinking about him now?*

Their eyes met awkwardly, and they broke the contact. He needed to get himself under control. This was work, for crying out loud. He was going to embolden all the other teachers who had looked at him significantly in the hallway today as if to say, you're going to be hearing about this later! Couldn't a single man invite a young, attractive woman to do an observation without raising suspicion? Apparently not.

And she was attractive... she had caught his notice that first Sunday, but she was becoming more beautiful to him every day. Ava had an inner beauty which shone through every feature. A thoughtfulness, gentleness. He thought about the way that she had gripped Elizabeth's fingers after her fall, looking like she was about to cry over another person's pain. About the way that she leaned over each of his students now, eager to lend a hand, smiling over their successes as if solving a fraction was equivalent to winning the Nobel Prize. *How could she ever think that she wouldn't be an amazing teacher?*

He was only noticing all these things because he was stuck obsessing over someone he couldn't have. She snuck into his thoughts more than he cared to admit. *That's what happens when your days drag on, hour after hour, alone,* he thought. *It's hard to keep those unwanted thoughts from bubbling up to the surface.* Someone like Ava, she'd get snatched up eventually. And based on Jess's comments to her husband at the beach, some guy was already trying to do just that. Pete comforted himself with his mantra of late: *Then, she'd be Gone.*

Because Ava had arrived later in the day than expected, it wasn't long before they had to break for lunch. Pete lined the students up at the door and then motioned for Ava to join him as they walked to the cafeteria.

"Did you bring a lunch?" he asked.

"No. I had one packed and ready to go in the refrigerator, but of course I forgot it in my hurry to get here this morning."

"No worries. You can buy a student lunch, if you don't mind chicken nuggets."

She shrugged, saying, "Beggars can't be choosers." Pete waited for her as she walked through the line and collected a juice cup, a cluster of grapes, and a small bag of crinkle-cut fries on a Styrofoam tray. It was funny to see her standing in line next to all the little kids. Layla invited her to eat with them, but Ava politely declined.

"Your class is so welcoming," Ava grinned as she rejoined Pete.

He led the way back to his classroom and explained, "You're a big hit. They love it when new people visit, especially because they're so worn out at the end of the year."

Pete let Ava sit at his desk again and unwrapped his peanut butter and jelly sandwich on a side table instead.

If Pete was honest, he was enjoying her visit, too. It beat scrolling through basketball stats and news articles like he usually did on his lunch break.

Before he dug in, Pete asked, "Do you want me to ask the blessing?"

"Sure," said Ava.

They bowed their heads. "Father, thank You for bringing Ava here today. I ask that You would guide her as she thinks about what to do next in her career, and I pray that we all may be protected as we go about our day. Please bless this food to our bodies, in Jesus's name, Amen."

Ava thanked him, and Pete nodded, clearing his throat. He didn't like praying in front of other people, but he felt a strong sense of duty to do so—a duty born of gratitude. Even the classroom walls around Pete reminded him how God had brought him to this high-quality school in a beautiful state. *With a beautiful girl,* Pete added against his will.

Isabelle had used her beauty like a weapon, distracting him from all of his wiser intentions. And here he was—supposedly reformed and trying to stay objective—having warm and fuzzy feelings with Ava sitting mere inches away.

He had started to forget that he was at work, the way she brightened the place up. Ava's hair was loose and wavy today; she half-laughed once she noticed him looking at her and cast her gaze to the floor.

Why in the world does she seem so insecure? Pete wondered. If he were as attractive as Ava, he would be strutting around like he owned the place, not trying to blend into the background. Her humility was just another quality that made Ava unique.

"Met any interesting people since you've moved?" Pete asked aggressively, worried that he would start outright flirting if things continued the way they were going. If mentally reminding himself that Ava was bad news wasn't going to work, he might as well draw out the proof for his own ears.

"Yes," she said. "Of course, everyone is friendly at church. My boss is nice, and I've made a few friends at work now." Her smile widened at the thought and Pete saw her glance down at her phone.

She must be waiting on a text from her boyfriend. There it was. The reminder that Pete needed to stay away. Confident that he was out of any danger, and satisfied that he had been right after all, Pete didn't even mind making small talk with Ava for the rest of the afternoon. She was a great girl, for whoever this guy was. But not for Pete.

10

Thursday evening at work, Jenny tasked Ava with straightening the far end of the store before closing time—the end of the store where Jackson was standing, bored out of his mind next to an empty register. It was unlikely that they'd see many more customers tonight, but they had thirty more minutes to act like they would.

Jackson's posture straightened when he saw Ava coming toward him. They had exchanged a few playful glances across the room earlier in the day, but they hadn't yet had a chance to talk without interruption. "Finally," he said, his eyes sweeping the area to make sure they were alone. "I have some news."

"News?" Ava asked, heart pounding.

His grin expanded. "I got accepted into the program."

Ava squealed and gave him a quick hug before remembering where she was. She stepped back. "Congratulations!"

Jackson shook his head. "It's all because of you. You don't know how long I've been waiting for this." He produced a small velvet box from his pocket.

"Jackson," Ava breathed. Images of their future together flashed through her head—the tearful goodbye at the airport where he would promise to think of her every moment that he was away, the hours that they would spend talking on the phone, their relationship growing deeper and deeper until they were reunited at last, never to be parted again.

Jackson cracked the box open; two diamond earrings twinkled

69

inside.

"Oh," Ava reached out a hand. "They're beautiful."

"You like them?"

"I *love* them."

"Need me to hold them for you until our shift's over?" he asked.

"Are you kidding, I'm never letting these go!" Ava snatched the box from him and hid it behind her back as proof. "Besides, I'm wearing a dress with pockets. Best invention known to womankind."

Jackson spied their boss on her way over, and turned to reorganize the business cards. Ava floated away to arrange the hangers by size. When Jenny paused mid-course to talk with Mariana, Jackson rejoined Ava.

"How was your observation yesterday?" he asked, a little too casually.

"Great! Pete really knows what he's doing. I was able to pick up a few new ideas from him."

"That's good."

"So, what time do you have to be at your friend's house tomorrow?"

"My friend's house?"

Ava cocked her head to the side. "Your friend. You said you had to help him move?"

"Oh yeah. He's really disorganized—I probably won't know the time until the last minute."

"That stinks."

"Yeah." Jackson looked back across the store to make sure Jenny wasn't watching. "Hey," he whispered. "Put your earrings in, I want to see them on you."

Ava shook her head at him and furtively put on the jewelry, tossing her hair behind her ears. "How do they look?"

"Gorgeous." Jackson leaned toward her, and Ava swatted him away. "Get back to work," she said, and set her mind to do the same, still feeling the heat of his gaze behind her.

# # #

Friday night, Isaac parked the van on the street outside the Markham house, as there were already several cars in the driveway. Ava got out, never ceasing to marvel at how warm it still was at 6:30

in the evening. She looked up at the cream-colored exterior of the home, surprised to see it was two stories—a less common design around Florida. Pale blue plumbago bushes softened the edges of a walnut-stained front porch.

Isaac hoisted a carton of pop on his shoulder and they headed to the door. Ava knocked, and was greeted by Mrs. Markham.

"Hey," Joy said. "I'm so glad you could make it!"

"Thank you for having us," Ava replied.

"Come on in and make yourselves at home! There's some appetizers on the coffee table. Isaac, you can put the sodas out here." She led Isaac through a spacious kitchen and out onto the back patio. Ava meandered after him, not realizing until it was too late that Noah (and therefore Jess) had not followed—they had come in behind her and parked in the living room next to a bowl full of chips.

Joy set out a cooler for Isaac to load the pop into, and disappeared into the kitchen. Ava greeted Jon, who was watching hot dogs and burgers sizzle on a gas grill while chatting with Pete. The smell was heavenly, and the weather didn't even feel all that hot thanks to the twin ceiling fans circulating above them.

"Ava." Pete nodded to her cordially, reclining in a green patio chair.

"Pete," Ava echoed, sinking into a loveseat opposite him.

Pete turned back to Jon to continue their conversation. "You're just making popcorn, man, not saving the world. Give yourself a break, alright?"

"I just want to do a good job," Jon muttered. He eyed the smoking meat. "That should be good." He transferred it all onto a large cookie sheet. Pete leaned over to open the glass door for him, and Jon took the food inside.

Isaac took a seat next to Ava. "What was that all about?" he asked Pete.

"Jon started his first job this week. He's got some youthful insecurity about it, that's all."

The first time Ava ever saw Pete, he was advising Jon about how to deal with "these girls" that seemed to want nothing more in their life than to shop and be amused. This second dismissal—this time of teenage behavior—also hit a nerve.

"Why is everyone so down on young people?" she burst.

"What?"

She mimicked sayings she had heard all her life: "You're too young, you wouldn't understand, you can't make a difference."

"That's not what I said." Pete answered, seeming blindsided.

"Just because someone is young doesn't mean they aren't mature, or driven…"

"Yeah, there are exceptions to every rule. Anyway, calling someone inexperienced isn't an insult."

"But shouldn't you be mindful of the exceptions before slapping a label on somebody?"

"Sure, I could run around terrified of insulting someone, and not say anything at all."

That approach worked pretty well for her. "At least what you would say would be worthwhile then!"

He sighed. "Did Jon seem upset to you?"

"No," she acknowledged.

"That's because we're friends. I give him a hard time, and he knows I'm acting normal."

"You do know that it's possible to be caring and normal at the same time?"

"Or I could be honest and offer solutions to problems. That is caring about someone."

Ava huffed. She guessed that she could sort of see his point. It was clear that he cared about Jon, she would give him that.

"Don't worry, you'll understand this when you're older." His mouth twitched, holding back a laugh.

"I'm twenty-three!" she shouted.

"My point exactly."

"That's it." She pulled her phone out from her bag and searched the Internet for Jeremiah Chapter 1. She read aloud, emphatically, punctuating the particularly relevant words with hand gestures: "But the Lord said unto me, Say not, I am a child: for thou shalt go to all that I shall send thee, and whatsoever I command thee thou shalt speak." She leveled her gaze at him. *Yeah. I went there.*

He paused. "Well, I will say that I've never been quoted at from the book of Jeremiah before."

"Seems like twenty-three-year-olds are good company to keep, after all."

"Guys, guys, I'm still here." Ava started at the sight of Isaac, cracking up beside her. "Can we go get some food now?"

She looked at Pete and smiled, a little embarrassed that she got so carried away. Pete stood and opened the door again. "After you."

On the marble kitchen island, the Markhams had put together an amazing spread. Jon said a word of prayer and they filed around the table. Ava added cheese, grilled onions, and lettuce to her hamburger, and was about to squirt ketchup over her hot dog when Pete exclaimed behind her, "What are you doing?"

"What are you talking about?"

"Putting ketchup on your hot dog? You're going to ruin it!"

"Are you serious? What else would you put on it?"

He gave her a sainted look and recited: "mustard, onions, relish, pickle, tomatoes, sport peppers and celery salt."

"Obviously," she smirked. "Can you even fit all that on there?"

He broke open a bun and demonstrated to the best of his ability (based on the toppings he had available). "I'll ask Jon to be more prepared next time," he said.

My goodness, she thought. *The man is even arrogant about his food!* It was hard for Ava to maintain her high moral ground when, a few minutes later, she lifted her hot dog to her lips and a dollop of ketchup fell onto her light pink tank. She wanted to crawl under the couch, but on the outside, she dabbed the stain unconcernedly with a napkin. Pete's insufferable grin showed that he wasn't fooled a bit.

"So, what game do you guys want to play tonight?" Jon asked the group, who had all since filtered into the living room.

Pete groaned. "We're adults. Can't we make conversation without having some sort of pre-planned activity?"

"You're just scared you're going to get beat," Jon said.

"You know that's not true."

"Do you have any trivia games?" Ava asked. Knowledge or word-based games were her specialty.

"Sure," Jon said, pulling out a gaming controller. *Oh,* Ava thought. *That kind of game.*

"Who else is playing?" Jon asked. "We can add up to six people." He turned on the console and opened up the program. Cheery game-show music filled the room.

"I'm down," Isaac said.

"Pass," Jess said from Ava's side. She was busy trying to keep Noah entertained with the books that she brought in her diaper bag for him, rather than with the glass candle burning in the middle of the coffee table which he kept scooting closer and closer to.

Amber and her girls agreed to be a team, and Jake signed up as well. After a short pause with no more volunteers, Jon filled in his own name, and Pete's.

"Really?" Pete said.

"It's better when more people play," Jon explained.

"Just remember, you did this to yourself." Pete cracked his knuckles together. It was his turn first.

The question read, "What particles make up the nucleus of an atom?"

Easy, protons and neutrons, Ava thought. They passed the controller around. She, Isaac, and Pete picked the right answer from the list of options.

She was the best at the entertainment and arts questions but missed a few social studies questions. Before long, she and Pete had racked up so many points that they were the only two contenders left. The gentle chatter of all the other houseguests had faded and the room seemed riveted by the competition before them.

The screen read, "Final Round!"

She laughed at the first question: "Who wrote *The Count of Monte Cristo?*"

She immediately hit Alexandre Dumas. Pete, after some stalling, made an incorrect guess.

"Don't feel bad. You're going against an English major," she told him.

The next question humbled her a bit. "The first ever Superbowl winner was..." *umm, the New England Patriots?*

Pete shook his head. "The Green Bay Packers! How could you not know that?"

She made a face at him, and the final question flashed on the screen — "What is the capital of Iceland?"

Ava groaned. *Really? Why does it have to be a geography question!*

Pete answered with confidence, and Ava fell for the distractor answer.

Their audience cheered as the television flashed Pete's name, proclaiming him as the winner. Ava burned. She was *not* used to losing quiz games. "Reykjavík? Who's ever heard of that?"

Pete just grinned, letting her answer her own question.

His victorious smile haunted Ava all the way home.

Her sulking did not escape Jess's notice. "You and Pete sure took over the game for those last few minutes," she said.

"Don't remind me," Ava said, crossing her arms.

"Maybe it was fueled by some leftover tension from your debate on the back patio," Isaac suggested. *Traitor!* Ava thought.

"Debate?" Jess asked, turning around in the passenger seat to face Ava.

Ava sighed, looking at Noah's sleeping form beside her to calm herself down. His pudgy fists were curled over his seatbelt in the most adorable way, and his head lolled to one side. "It was just Pete being irritating," she said. "Nothing new there."

"What did he say to make you mad?"

"Why are you assuming that I'm the one who lost my temper?"

"So you weren't?"

Ava muttered, "He just thinks that he is so much better than everyone else. Talking down to younger people."

"He was talking down to you?"

Isaac said, "Actually, Pete was talking very highly of you the other day."

That piqued Ava's attention. "What?"

"At Bible study. I was asking him how your observation went, and he didn't have enough good things to say about you. He said that you were attentive, and got along well with the kids."

"And that I was late," Ava guessed, though Pete's compliments had taken the bite out of her tone.

"You were?" Isaac said, turning the van onto their street. "He didn't mention that at all."

"Oh."

Jess leaned closer. "If you weren't still obsessed with Jackson, I would accuse you of being into Pete right now."

"What? No way. Not in a million years. Have you met the two of us?"

She leaned back, satisfied with Ava's response. "You're just a little defensive, that's all."

"I am defensive against the insanity that has momentarily taken over your body. You have nothing to worry about when it comes to a relationship—" Ava spat the last word out, "—between Pete and I."

"Okay," Jess threw her palms up in defense. "You're not into Pete. How is Mr. Wonderful, then?"

Ava ran her thumb over her blank phone screen, which she had been eyeing every couple of minutes. "Strangely quiet."

"I'm sure it's nothing. But if it is something...." Jess punched a fist into her opposite palm, which was no more intimidating than back when she used to threaten Ava's former boyfriend. Still, the fierceness in Jess's eyes made Ava smile. Nothing could hit Ava too hard with Jess around. She'd just have to be careful and keep up that confidence when she was alone.

11

Ava tried not to look at her phone. Tried, and failed miserably, like she had been for her whole Saturday night. She opened her messages app, just to make sure that she hadn't missed anything. *Nope.* She had sent the last text a full twenty-two hours ago: three sentences long, complete with two emojis, in reply to Jackson's one-word comment of "yeah." She powered her phone off and plugged it in so that she wouldn't text back a second time when she had already left him plenty of fodder for conversation...or so she had thought.

She didn't want to be that girl anymore who agonized over every message, who lived and breathed by her phone and took offense to a person's silence when, for all intents and purposes, Jackson was likely very busy. Yet, he had already told her that he would be doing "nothing much" (two words) this weekend. And until recently, *he* had initiated long talks, with prompting such as "you fascinate me" and "I want to get to know you." Somehow, it had all changed. Had she done something wrong?

She groaned and reached over to her journal, just to have some distraction. She rolled over to her stomach and crossed her legs in the air, sliding her pen out of its holder. Mom had bought Ava the beautiful leather-bound journal for her birthday several years back, noticing how Ava preferred to have paper with her when she jotted down notes from the Bible, or saw something that she wanted to remember. She wasn't as faithful at filling up the pages as she wanted to be, and had only recently rediscovered it as she was packing to go to Florida.

She laughed at the first page, penned after a sleepover with Jess. "Must-haves in a guy: Dark hair. Light eyes. Taller than me. Kills spiders!!!" Jackson certainly met the first three qualifications. She was fairly certain he would satisfy the fourth, seeing as just the other day in Hydrangea, he had speedily dispatched a lizard who had scurried under the register. *With his bare hand!* She shuddered and flipped forward to the next blank page.

Ok, might as well give the list a refresh, she thought, remembering the suggestion that Amber had made to her on the beach. Ava's pen hovered above the paper. It was one thing to write out all the fun things that she wished or dreamed of. It was more daunting to think about what she wanted in her future spouse. Ava closed her eyes. *God,* she breathed. *You've told me in Your word that You know the way that I take... please help me to see Your hand in this. Or...* the familiar fear gripped her stomach. *I'm so blessed, Lord, and I don't have room to complain. If I can serve You better by being single, I ask for Thy will to be done. In Jesus's name, Amen.*

She felt calmer, as she often did after praying from her heart, and felt the closeness with God that she'd been missing recently. *Ok,* she thought. *I can do this.* "My Dating Expectations..." she printed as the title. "Reliability." Of course she had to write this in bulleted list format. Space down, indent. "Being on time, keeping dates and returning calls."

Next, "Leadership." For the description she wrote, "Being the initiator, someone who seeks me out and shows that he cares about being with me." Leadership seemed to be a real struggle for her first boyfriend. It was like he was with her for convenience's sake, and she had to convince him to want to spend time with her.

Which brought her to the next quality: "Thoughtfulness." She tried not to scratch that one too hard into the paper. Something that she thought she had found in Jackson, but that had inexplicably dropped away. "Honesty. Being straightforward with one's intentions." Ava wished that she knew where her and Jackson's relationship—if she could even call it that—was going.

She could take it if he was losing interest in her. But the wondering, the not knowing, was killing her. Something wasn't right, and she hoped he'd come clean soon. "Compassion." If she could only be valued, listened to. Ava snapped the book shut with a sigh, wondering, *Why are all these starting to sound the same?*

God, she prayed, *my identity is in You. I know that You have formed me and redeemed me, and that You want me to be respected. Please protect me, and heal this ache that I feel inside.*

# # #

Sunday morning, Pete was standing in the church lobby when Ava walked in.

"Hey, how're you doing?" she asked, seeming as cheerful as ever. Her long black skirt swished against her legs.

"Fine."

"Just fine?" Her brow furrowed at his standard monotone.

"Yep." Pete didn't like to sugarcoat things. He wasn't the type to sit around and think about how happy he was every minute of the day. *Up until about a month ago.*

"This is for you," Ava declared, handing him a red envelope with his name written on the front.

"What's this?"

"A thank you note, for letting me come and see your class this week. I really appreciate it."

He laughed. "You didn't have to do that. Thanks, that's sweet."

She shrugged, smiled, and headed for the sanctuary. Pete walked to his row, and sat in the third seat from the right. He slid his arm over the empty chair next to him and couldn't help but glance back at Ava. She was happily seated with Jess's family, surrounded with new friends. Everyone loved her already.

He shook his head and reached forward for a songbook. The song leader called "Be Thou My Vision," and Pete sang along tunelessly. He wasn't really into singing, but knew that God didn't care about missed notes and deserved his worship.

He followed along with the week's message in his Bible, using the church bulletin as a bookmark. The inside of the folded pamphlet contained a list of upcoming dates. On the back were lines to write on, but Pete never was one for notetaking. God had blessed him with a sharp memory in that once he heard something for the first time, it stuck with him forever. Today's sermon was about having faith in God through trials, like David did when he was chased by King Saul.

When David was tempted to take matters into his own hands in anger or pride, he remembered that God would take care of him and make things right.

Hasn't God taken care of me so far? Pete thought. He went through his mental checklist of all the dreams that he'd had which were now fulfilled, just like he always did when he needed to re-anchor his thoughts. God had brought him to this amazing place, and blessed him with an unbelievably good school to work at. He had an understanding boss, and great students. He was living on his own, paying his bills, and wanted for nothing. So, Pete had to stop stressing about what was "missing" in his life. If the Lord wanted him to be married, he would send the right woman along in His time.

This he knew. What he felt was a different matter completely.

Pete had survived life by working hard. The more jobs he picked up in high school, college, and even after he got his full-time position, the more stable he felt. The less he worried about missing out on relationships, or his family's uncertain finances. But standing still and waiting? Trusting that God could strike a love in his heart for a woman who would stay, or else strengthen Pete as he lived the rest of his life alone? That wasn't something he could ever see himself feeling one-hundred percent comfortable with. Comfortable or not, that was what he had to do. He just had to believe, like in David's life, that his own story would come to a happy end.

After service ended, Pete meandered over to talk with his brother — and instantly regretted it.

"You and Ava were pretty evenly matched last night, huh?"

"Yeah, she's smart," Pete admitted.

Ivy ran up and pulled on her father's pant leg. "Daddy? I have to go potty."

Jake shot Pete a harried look but took his daughter's hand and set off.

Pete followed them in the direction of the fellowship hall, hoping to catch Jon for some sports talk. He bumped into Ava instead, who was hurrying out of the bathroom, looking disappointed.

"Sorry," she cried. "I have to go. No one took my shift today, but I'm just thankful it was an afternoon shift!"

He couldn't help himself. "Don't be late," he scolded.

She shot him a stern look, but it was softened a little by what he thought might be shame at her "big mess-up" on Wednesday. He hoped she knew that it hadn't really mattered at all. After observing her consistency over the past few weeks, Pete knew that he could count on Ava Keller more than he could count on most people. As an acquaintance.

"Bye!" she called over her shoulder. The glass door swung shut behind her shrinking form, and his heart sunk.

God, why do I keep having these feelings for her when I need to let them go? I've tried being with a woman before who I know I had no business being in a relationship with. And Ava seems different... he thought about her quick wit, about how she quoted from a book of the Bible so easily that many people hadn't even read. *But that will only make it more painful when she finds who and what she's looking for.*

It would be easier if she would start bringing her boyfriend around. Or if she would just move back to Iowa already. But for the time being, she was here. She kept coming back. And standing there, still staring at the closed door, Pete found himself wondering how many more times he would be able to watch Ava walk away.

12

Monday night, Pete's phone buzzed on the kitchen counter. He slapped down a frozen pizza, still in its plastic wrapping, and opened up a text from Jon.

Jon: SOS!

Pete shook his head. If Jon had something important to say, he would have called. More than likely, Jon had just got off work and wanted to get a good session of gaming in.

Pete: What?

Jon: You have to come to the theater NOW. Ava is here, with the most beautiful girl I have ever seen!

This was big. Jon was risking Pete's ridicule by telling him about a girl he liked?

Pete: Sorry, I'm busy.

Jon: No you're not.

Pete: Why does everyone assume that I'm never busy?!

Jon: Because you never are. Come on, man! I'll owe you big time.

Pete considered the wisdom of voluntarily appearing at a date-like place where Ava was.

Pete: What sort of bribe do you have in mind?

Jon: Comped popcorn, soda, and candy. I know you like those chocolate chip things.

Pete: Make it a large combo and have it ready for me when I get there. Extra butter.

Pete sighed, turned off the oven, and returned the pizza to the freezer. He eyed his stained and beat-up gray tee, deciding to trade it in for a tan shirt that was more presentable, and slipped on his sandals. No use staring at the mirror—this was as good as it was going to get.

The movie theater was only five minutes away from his apartment. It featured showtimes on an old-time marquee, topped with magenta curlicues. He parked and headed into the lobby, spotting Jon dancing anxiously by the concession stand. Jon had changed out of his theater uniform and had Pete's promised snacks waiting. He shoved the soda and popcorn into Pete's arms, and then dropped the candy box on top with a pile of napkins. "Let's go!"

Pete had no time to take in "the most beautiful girl Jon had ever seen!" because he spotted Ava standing next to the newcomer, her head thrown back laughing. Her golden hair was pulled into a high ponytail and she wore dangly earrings that bobbed when she moved. Her eyes glittered just like her sequined top. Pete swallowed hard and worked to regain his composure.

"Ava," Jon called. "What are you doing here?"

"Catching a movie," Ava stated the obvious. "This is my friend, Mariana." Mariana's long, thick black hair swung down in stark contrast to her white sundress. Her eyelashes fluttered up at Jon, who was smiling like an idiot.

"It's a pleasure to meet you." Jon stuck out his hand and Pete groaned internally. But Mariana didn't seem to notice the cheesiness of Jon's introduction.

"You too," she said.

Ava rested a hand on Pete's arm and he actually flinched! *You moron,* he berated himself. She lowered her fingers and pretended not to notice. "These are my friends from church, Jon and Pete."

"What movie are you going to see?" asked Mariana.

"Well, uh..." Jon glanced at the girls' tickets, resting on an antique arcade game. "What a coincidence! We're going to see *So in Love with You* too."

"Huh. That is crazy." Ava cocked her head at Pete. "Where are your tickets?"

"Oh, I was just waiting for Pete to get here," Jon said. "He's paying tonight. Lost a bet."

He winked at Pete and Pete resisted the urge to knock his stupid grin right off of his face, shooting him a look that he hoped communicated, *Free movie tickets for a year.*

Pete mumbled the movie title to the cashier, paid, and returned to the trio. Jon was asking, "Since we're all going to see the same movie, do you mind if we sit with you guys?"

"Not a problem," Ava said. "Right?" she asked, looking at Pete.

Something about the way she constantly loved to challenge him made him want to demolish her pride and kiss her all at the same time.

"Makes sense," he shrugged instead.

"So," she turned, leading the way to Theater Two. "Are you a big Annalise Carver fan?"

"The biggest," Pete replied. He might not have been a rom-com buff, but he'd have to live under a rock to not know the Hollywood starlet.

"Really interesting concept isn't it? Mixing romance with the zombie apocalypse?"

Maybe this movie wouldn't be half bad. "Yep."

"Ha!" Ava turned on him. "This movie is about high-school sweethearts who reconnect at sea. So, what are you two really doing here?"

Pete tossed his head over his shoulder at Jon and Mariana, now several feet behind them, deep in conversation.

"Ah," Ava said. "You know, that might work. Mari is a really sweet girl."

"And Jon's a good kid."

"Seems like it. Young or not," Ava shoved Pete playfully.

They came through the door of the dark theater. Willing to help her friend out, Ava remained on Pete's right side as she scooted into a middle row, letting Jon and Mari sit together. Even though Jon had deprived Pete of his supper, Pete offered Ava some of his popcorn. Their hands brushed the soda at the same time and Pete forced his hands to his lap. The next two hours were misery, and not just because the movie was terrible.

As soon as the lights went down, the tension rose. He found himself wishing that it was just him and Ava there, that he could brush his fingers over her wrist, put an arm around her. He saw her shake with laughter out of the corner of his eye during the corny gags, and put her hand over her mouth during one of those ridiculous, overdone proclamations of love. At least she didn't cry.

As the credits rolled, Ava picked up her purse. "What did you think?"

"What a surprise," he replied. "The beautiful girl somehow never found anyone to go out with her until she met the good-looking guy in the middle of the movie. Then they lived happily ever after."

"You can't really go in to one of these movies expecting to be surprised. It's the familiarity that's so great about it. It makes you feel good."

"Maybe it makes *you* feel good," Pete answered. "It puts me to sleep."

Ava was wearing high heels that thumped every time that she walked. They made her almost as tall as him. She looked evenly into his eyes as if to say, "You're impossible."

She jumped suddenly, and started feeling around for something in her bag. She pulled out her phone and her face fell.

"What's wrong?" he asked.

"Nothing," Ava said. "It's just spam."

"You seem pretty upset over getting spam."

She glanced at the movie posters on the walls, then up at the ceiling. Her voice was tight. "It's not what I got that's upsetting me. It's what

85

I'm not getting."

"Tell me." Pete didn't know why he was being so pushy, but suddenly he had to know. He had an unsettled feeling that wouldn't be righted until he had figured out what was going on.

"It's stupid."

"Ava," he growled.

"It's just this guy," she threw her hands up. "See? Now you're going to think that I'm getting all caught up like one of my sappy movie heroines."

Pete tried to recall the last time he had heard someone use the word "heroine" in casual conversation. He shook his head, "Listen, I know I can come off as judgmental, but I do want to help. Is this guy treating you all right?"

"He was, but now I don't know where we stand. He doesn't seem that interested in me anymore." She dug circles into the carpet with the heel of her shoe.

Anger burned in Pete's gut. "Then he's an idiot." She looked up at him to see if he was joking. He wasn't.

"What?"

"Any guy that wouldn't want to talk to you, spend time with you, or keep you happy is an idiot, and you deserve better." *Where did that come from?* Pete thought. He hadn't meant to sound so intense. But it was the truth. He would kill to have a girlfriend like Ava, and this guy was wasting his chance with her. Stupid behavior frustrated Pete to no end. He didn't know Ava's boyfriend personally, but considering the fact that he was stringing along someone as nice as her, he was willing to bet that this guy was not only stupid—he was scum.

"Thanks," Ava said with a cautious smile.

Jon and Mariana caught up with them and Ava widened her smile, wiping all signs of hurt from her face. "Ready to go?" she asked.

"Yeah," Mariana replied. She turned to Jon, leaning shyly to one side. "So, I'll talk to you later?"

"You bet," Jon said.

"Thanks guys. This was...fun." Ava said, stepping backwards toward the exit. "See you Wednesday."

"See ya." Jon and Pete watched them walk out, and Jon looked so happy, Pete didn't even rail on him for making him see (and pay for) the stupid movie. At the memory of how stunning Ava looked, and the way it felt to have her seated close by his side, Pete thought, *Maybe it wasn't such a bad idea after all.*

# # #

Once she was back at the Wilsons', the more Ava thought about the movie, the more she wondered about Pete's behavior. *Why does he care so much about Jackson freezing me out?*

She debriefed with Jess in the kitchen. Her friend was up late, chopping up and packing fresh fruit for Noah's babysitter to use through the rest of the week.

"It sounds to me like he's into you," Jess told Ava.

"No way. Pete? You're over-romanticizing again."

The accusation didn't affect Jess in the slightest. Instead, she let out a contented sigh and mused, "I didn't realize that Pete could be so sensitive."

Ava snorted. "Pete?" she repeated. But Ava had to admit, she was touched by how upset he looked when he found out that Jackson had hurt her feelings. It was nice that *somebody* cared about the way she was feeling, even if it wasn't the somebody who she most wanted to hear from.

"He's a good guy," Ava continued. "But we are definitely just friends." "Friends" was a good place for them to be, considering that "I can't stand you" was where they had started.

"I've got to stay busy though. Going out tonight was good for me. I can't mope around wondering when Jackson is going to text me all day every day."

Jess pointed the knife in Ava's direction, "Tomorrow, you should go on that run you keep talking about."

Ava dropped her forehead down on the granite countertop. "Yeah, I should," she moaned. Ava was not a fitness junkie, and she sometimes had a hard time working up the motivation to exercise. *But stress-relieving endorphins sound pretty good about now,* Ava thought. Jess slid a few strawberries her way as a peace offering.

"Thanks," Ava raised her head and took the snack. She looked at Jess's growing collection of plastic baggies. "Is it hard, being away from Noah during the day?"

"It's the worst. But I'm glad he's well-taken care of while I'm gone."

Jess put down the knife. "I'm thinking of opening up my own salon one day, so that he can hang out with me more."

Jess had successfully turned her adolescent passion for fixing all her friends' hair before their school dances into a 10-to-6 job as a hairdresser, and, with her talent in color and style, Ava knew Jess had a promising future as a business owner.

Ava told her, "You could make one here, put a chair and mirror in your spare room. If I ever move out, that is."

"Don't you dare feel like there is any hurry. I love having you back around. But an in-home salon is an idea. I have picked up a few regular customers."

"I am so proud of you," Ava said.

"Likewise!"

"What have I done that you would be proud of me for?" Sometimes her negativity bubbled up before Ava even knew it.

Jess put a hand on her hip, counting the reasons out: "Taking a leap of faith, carving a path for yourself... don't sell yourself short. I know that you can't wait to get a job and get married, and I don't blame you. But don't wish this transitional time away, either. The more milestones I go through, the more I realize that there are blessings during each of them."

Ava rested her chin in her hands. "When did you get so old and wise?"

Jess stuck her tongue out in response. "I've always been old and wise. Or have you forgotten that I am a whole ten months older than you?"

"You may be older, but you're also the crazy one."

"True. Look!" she held up a strawberry that she had cut into a heart shape. "All the best artists are a little bit crazy."

"That is adorable. Be sure to save a few more of those for me in the morning." Ava groaned, thinking about what the first run would be like after a five-month leave of absence from exercise. "I'm going to need sustenance."

"Don't forget to lay out your workout clothes. Having them ready will help you get going."

"I will. I'm going to get up early, before the sun gets too hot. Want to come with?"

Jess made a face. "No way. I get enough exercise running after Noah. I'll be sending you moral support from my sleep."

"Oh, thanks."

Ava needed all the moral support she could get. She hoped that the run would prove to be a useful distraction, although she was skeptical that it would help much. Ava hugged Jess goodnight, got ready for bed, put on her most comfortable cotton PJs, and turned out the light. After sinking into her mattress and sneaking one last peek at her phone, Ava put it facedown and went to sleep.

13

Ava's pulse beat along with the music as her feet pounded over the endless sidewalk. She would make it to the church and take a break on the front step before jogging back to Jess and Isaac's. Breathe in, breathe out. Physically and mentally, working out was a time for Ava to refresh and refocus, so although it had been hard to drag herself out of bed, Ava was glad she'd come. *I am strong. I am beautiful*—her thoughts were interrupted when a fat rain droplet hit her arm. She halted her pump-up session, looking skyward. *I am wet?*

Ava should have turned back when she saw the storm clouds roll in ten minutes ago, but she thought she could make it to her milestone in time. Not so. It didn't take long for the heavens to pour out completely, pelting down on her so effectively that she didn't even try to run anymore. Instead, she sheltered her phone and earbuds with her hands as she scanned her surroundings for any kind of cover.

Ava walked parallel to a series of sand-colored condominiums, many of which had sweeping front porches. *Maybe if I could find the clubhouse, I could stand under the overhang...* she stopped short. Two condos away from her sat Pete and Rosalie. Pete's pint-sized niece was scribbling a drawing in pink sidewalk chalk, jabbering on while her uncle reclined on a lawn chair. Pete and Ava locked eyes and she waved feebly, quickening her pace to join the pair on the patio.

"Ava!" Rosalie shouted, hopping up and throwing her small arms around Ava's knees.

"Hey Rose! Careful, I'll get you all wet."

90

"I was just thinking about you this morning! I was praying that you and Uncle Pete would..."

"Rose," Pete cut her off. "Do you know where the towels are?"

"Yes. I'll go get one for Ava." She skipped away.

"Going for a run on a Florida summer afternoon. Not a good idea." Pete said grimly.

"I'm glad you were here," Ava admitted. He had told her that he lived close to the church early in her stay while inviting her out of courtesy to join some of the other church members to watch basketball. At the time, she never thought that she would come and visit.

Rosalie reappeared with a worn-out cream towel. As Ava dried her face, she noticed that she was leaving streaks of black mascara on the cloth. *So embarrassing.* "Thanks," she told them both.

"Don't mention it," Pete said. A timer went off inside, its chimes echoing through the screen door. "Dinner's ready," he told Rosalie. He turned to Ava. "Come on inside."

"No, it's okay. I'm sure it will stop soon." She shifted her weight from side to side. It was gusting so hard that some of the droplets were coming inside the patio now.

"I don't think so," Pete said. He opened the screen door and the smell of broth and herbs hit Ava, making her empty stomach growl involuntarily.

"If you insist," she conceded, and stepped inside the living room. The furnishings were sparse and mismatched but the place seemed tidy. When Pete passed by her to shut off the oven in the nearby tiny kitchen, she caught another scent—somewhere between citrusy and woodsy—and found herself remembering how she and Pete were thrown together last evening.

"What's for lunch?" she asked, to channel her thoughts into a more appropriate avenue.

"Chicken pot pie."

She saw the carrot shavings, flour leavings, and rotisserie bag full of picked-over bones. "Homemade? I'm impressed!"

"It's Rosalie's favorite."

Rose chimed in, "I'm spending the day with Uncle Pete while Mom and Dad take Ivy to the doctor."

"I hope she's okay," Ava said.

"It's just a checkup." Pete spooned the steaming entrée into three small bowls. "But Jake and Amber both went because they like to take a special day with each of the girls from time to time."

"And Uncle Pete likes to have a special day with me!"

"That's right." Pete asked the blessing and they sat on bar stools, eating over his kitchen counter. Ava felt a little funny as her soaked feet dangled.

"What are you guys up to today?" She took a bite of the steaming dish and her taste buds sung. The biscuits on top were soft and flaky. "Wow, this is so good!"

"Thanks," Pete hunched his broad shoulders over his own bowl. "We're going to watch a movie."

"That sounds fun." Ava turned to Rose. "It must be nice to have an uncle who is such a good cook."

"Mm-hmm!" Rose nodded in-between bites. "Grandma taught him how."

"Did she teach your daddy too?"

Pete answered for her. "Jake didn't get as much time at home with my ma. She had to go back to work once our dad lost his job."

Ava put down her spoon. "That must have been hard."

Pete shrugged. "It was rough for a while, but we made it work. Things got easier once I got old enough to get a job myself."

"And look at you now! A world-class teacher." Ava smiled, but on the inside she felt troubled. All that she had to worry about in high school was getting one-hundred percents on her essays, and deciding what to wear to the next dance. She hadn't imagined that not everyone was lucky enough to have the same experience.

"No wonder you didn't want to teach high school," she spoke aloud, realizing belatedly that it might be rude.

"Worst time of my life," he grinned.

Ava shook her head. "So... why'd you choose a job where you're forced to be stuck in school forever?"

"I'm pretty good with younger kids," he said.

"Yep!" Rosalie seconded.

"I can't argue with that," Ava said. She scooped up one last stray pea from her bowl. "Are you going to whip us up some homemade apple pie now?"

"Next time," Pete replied, taking their dishes and putting them all in the sink. He walked to his small pantry and held up a box of pre-packaged snack cakes. "This is all you get."

Ava was relieved that Pete was finally showing some signs of being a normal bachelor. This new chef-babysitter image that she was adding to her mental file on him was seeming more and more bizarre by the minute.

"I'll take it to go," she said. Water squelched out of her shoes as she hopped off of her stool. "I have to go in to work this afternoon and should probably clean up a little."

Pete dropped the wrapped cake into her outstretched hand. His fingers were rough and warm. She quickly withdrew her own.

"Thank you so much for lunch. And shelter."

"Anytime."

She waved to Rosalie. "It was good to see you again, sweetie!"

"You too! See you later." After Pete inspected Rose's hands for pot pie residue, the wriggling girl hopped off her seat and ran to the couch, eager to work the remote.

"Have fun," Ava laughed as she saw Rosalie expertly navigate the channels until she settled on something with ponies and a lot of pink.

She could hear Pete's groan as she walked out the door.

# # #

Pete often went to the batting cages after work to blow off steam. Something about the steady *thwack* of the barrel against the ball made a day full of kid chatter and tardy bells disappear. Lately, though, his mind couldn't seem to stay empty. Even on summer vacation.

He thought about how Ava liked to twirl the end of her ponytail when she was talking. The pitching machine rattled.

How good she looked this afternoon sitting at his kitchen counter. *Plink.*

How he wanted to keep seeing her there, every afternoon for the rest of his life. *Whack.*

Of course, we'd move out eventually. Get a bigger place. Big enough for a couple of kids. The machine stalled. He was out of pitches. Pete dropped the bat, frustrated. What about Ava made him think about things that he had no right to think about? Expect things that he never had

93

expected before?

"Hey!"

Pete turned to see Isaac Wilson walking up to his cage. He waved him in.

"Hey," Pete sat down on a folding chair and pulled off his hat, wiping his sweaty brow with a towel.

"Mind if I join you?" Isaac asked.

"Not at all. I need a break anyway." Pete took a swig of water as Isaac dropped more coins into the pitching machine and took his place at bat.

"You know what you're doing," Pete said, watching Isaac drop into a textbook-worthy stance.

"Played all through high school," Isaac said. "I thought I'd take you up on your recommendation and check out the cages here."

"What position did you play?"

"Catcher. You know that's how Jess and I met?"

"Really?"

"Yeah." Isaac chuckled as he wound up for another hit. A swing and a miss.

"She was a year younger than me in school, but we had a few classes together. I was too shy to ever make a move. So Ava convinced her to go for team manager."

Isaac's next swing made contact. "Jess didn't know anything about baseball! I found out later that Ava gave her a crash course on the rules and drilled her on plays so that she could keep score. I'm glad she did. I drove Jess home a few nights after practice, and then Ava dropped some hints that I should ask her out. I figured since Ava was Jess's best friend, she would have a pretty good idea about how Jess felt. The rest is history."

Pete smirked, running his thumb down his beard. He could just see Ava intervening in her friend's love life. He used to think that she was as mild and sweet as could be, but he had seen firsthand her fire when he waded into issues that she was passionate about. And she was passionate about her friends.

"You know," Isaac said. "I always thought you and Ava would make a good match."

Pete sighed. He almost didn't feel like fighting it anymore. *Can't everybody see that I'm a grown man and I can handle my own relationships?* he thought. Even if he was a grown man at his breaking point.

"I think I drive her crazy," he said casually.

Isaac grinned. "My guess is that she's coming around."

"Yeah?" Isaac had known Ava for a long time, and his confidence left Pete wondering if he had a chance after all.

"I think this is my last pitch. Do you want to take over?" Isaac extended the end of the bat towards Pete.

"Thanks. Yeah, I think I do." Pete rose and steadied himself. He kept his eye on the ball and, *smack,* his bat reverberated with the impact. He watched the ball soar through the air and graze the netting at the top of the opposite end of the enclosure. As he clapped hands with Isaac, Pete thought about how good it felt to go for it.

Fighting for success in sports was easy. He had to give it his all to taste the excitement of victory. If he failed, he shook it off, trained, and went harder the next game. But fighting for Ava? Pete hated showing emotion in any way. He hated being vulnerable. He just wanted to shake off the weakness that she made him feel—a compulsion to love and protect that was beginning to permeate his daily rhythm.

Something told Pete that, once he gave in to his feelings for Ava, he would never be the same. Her loss would hurt even deeper than Isabelle's—of that, he was sure. Isabelle hadn't cared about him. He had thought that he was in love with her at the time, but, really, he wasn't. Pete realized that now as he thought about Ava's green eyes, that were not only beautiful, but constantly filled with gentleness toward others. Earlier that day, they had been filled with gentleness toward him, mourning a loss from his childhood that Pete hadn't ever had the luxury to cry over.

He had known how to respond when Isabelle started flirting with him for the first time. She was always straightforward with what she wanted. Pete didn't know if he could handle a girl with more delicate emotions. He didn't even know for sure if Ava was in to him at all.

She could just as easily be acting friendly, the same way that she treated everyone. At that thought, his head started to pound.

I have to stop pining, Pete said to himself, shaking out his shoulders. It was much safer to leave any thoughts of him and Ava getting together as far away as the last softball he had hit, lying discarded at the other end of the cages.

95

14

The church members' freeloading off of Pete's teacher discount seemed to have no end. Today's occasion was a reduced price to the county fair.

Of course, the fairgrounds couldn't possibly figure out a way to let him buy the tickets online, because that would make too much sense. Pete had to show up in person with his staff ID in order to get everyone in.

He cut his car's engine and walked up to the small crowd waiting for him at the entrance—Ava, Mariana, Jon, Will, and the girl Will had been bringing to church—all young people who had school or work off on a Tuesday morning. It didn't escape Pete's notice that they were also all couples, except for him and Ava. Even if the situation did throw them together, Ava looked relieved not to be the fifth wheel anymore as he approached.

Pete bought six purple wristbands from the kid at the counter, and swapped them for cash from the group.

"These wristbands are good for unlimited rides!" Jon said.

"That's because they get your money off the games and cheap merchandise instead," Pete commented.

"The games are all you'll get to do today. Still afraid of heights?"

"I'm not afraid of heights. These things just make me sick." Pete flicked his hand towards a tall drop attraction at the center of the fair.

"Your loss, man," Jon shrugged, following Pete's gaze. "I say we start with that one. What do you think?" He raised his eyebrows at

Mariana.

"Let's do it," she said.

Everyone turned to head to the attraction, but Ava hesitated. "What are you going to do if you're not going on any rides?" she asked Pete.

He glanced around and spotted a funnel cake truck. "I'm going to hang out over there. I'll meet up with you guys later."

As he started to walk away, Ava said, "Hold up," running to his side.

"I don't need a babysitter," he told her.

"I'm not going to let you sit here by yourself."

"You can go lose your breakfast with everyone else. I'm fine."

Ava ignored him, waving the two couples on who were hovering uncertainly near the entrance. "You might need a babysitter. You looked queasy a minute ago."

Pete acknowledged, "I am a baby when it comes to roller coasters."

"Even tiny ones?"

"Those are worse!" Pete said, stabbing a finger at the thin cables which held up the steel tracks of an oversized swing ride. "If I don't get sick, I'll have a headache for the rest of the day."

Ava's eyes trailed a guy who was walking away from the food truck, a funnel cake cradled between his hands. "Those look huge!"

"Do you want to split one?"

"Sure."

They stepped up to the counter and ordered their funnel cake with whipped cream and chocolate syrup on top.

Ava groaned, "Now *I'm* going to be sick."

They found a bench, and Pete shoveled his plastic fork into the dessert. "See? Now this is a good time."

Ava's phone pinged. "I'm not going to check it!" she said, clenching her jaw.

"Okay." Pete put his fork down, guessing that she was having the same non-committal guy problem that she told him about at the movie theater. "Can I ask you a question? And you can tell me if I need to mind my own business. But, why are you with somebody who makes you feel miserable?"

"I don't know, I'm probably just overthinking things. I'm trying to give Jackson some space. And, to be honest, I'm not really sure I am 'with him' at all. I mean, I thought I was."

"I think you should be able to tell," Pete said gently.

"I know."

Ava looked so defeated that Pete felt like wringing the guy's neck right then. *She's not your responsibility*, he reminded himself. Still, he couldn't help but see the similarities in Ava's situation and his own failed relationship. Pete had gotten over Isabelle's rejection with his sarcasm and a loud mouth, but now, Ava seemed to be physically folding in on herself. And she didn't deserve that.

"Eat some of this," Pete commanded. "If you leave it all to me, I'm going to get fat."

Ava giggled. "Okay."

"What else do you want to do while the others are gone?"

She looked around. "Aww, can we go see those animals?"

A handful of barnyard creatures meandered close by, behind a wooden gate. "Sure," Pete said, feigning enthusiasm. He was not an animal person. You didn't see too many sheep in the big city. Only bugs that crept in through the crevices of the older apartments. He could deal with it to cheer Ava up, though.

After the last bite, Pete threw away their oil-spotted paper plate and they walked together towards the small pasture, where a gray-haired woman was selling cups of feed.

"I'll take one, please," Ava said.

"Thank you very much. You kids have a good time now." Her eyes beamed at Pete, and he thought, *I know, I'm lucky to be hanging out with her.*

She probably assumed that they were a couple. It was starting to feel that way, as it was just the two of them spending time together.

Ava put her wallet away, as happy as could be.

Once the woman was out of earshot, Pete said, "See what I mean? This kind of stuff is how they rob you."

"It's worth it. Look how cute," Ava extended a hand full of grain to a miniature pony. She was stroking his nose when Pete felt a soft tug on his ankle. A goat was chewing on his shoelace! And liking it, apparently. The tugs got more aggressive as the goat got more and more of the lace in his mouth.

"Agh!" Pete shook his foot, and when that didn't work, he yanked his shoe off and pulled until the lace snapped back at him, dripping wet.

Ava was struggling to control a grin. "Sorry," she said, not looking sorry at all.

Pete walked a safe distance back to put on his shoe again. *Disgusting.* "Just keep that thing away from me."

"It's only a little goat!"

Pete eyed him warily. "I can't believe he's that hungry after standing around getting fed all day."

But Ava was so beautiful when she smiled that he didn't feel all that bad about being attacked by a stinking farm animal.

"Please. Tell me you're ready to move on now," he said.

"Sure." She sauntered away to the Midway section of the carnival, where every stand was the color of cotton candy, filled with squealing children intent upon winning a prize. The chipper organ music was deafening there.

He felt obligated to remind Ava, "You know you could buy one of those stuffed animals for a quarter of the price online."

She looked back at him and asked, "And where's the fun in that?"

Despite his grumblings, Pete was having a good time. Ava was so laid-back. She almost seemed like a kid herself, content to go along with anything. And that good-naturedness just kept stirring up the feelings of attraction that Pete couldn't seem to keep under control.

He glanced around. "Can I choose the activity this time?" he asked.

"Go ahead!"

Pete scanned all of the different booths. "Basketball." *Easy.*

Ava made a strangled noise.

"I thought you said I could pick."

She put her hands on her hips. "Sorry. You would pick the game that I'm going to be worst at."

"Water guns?" Pete suggested.

"That should be doable."

Pete gave the skater kid behind the counter two bucks, and he and Ava took their seats on a pair of low stools. Ava braced herself with both elbows rigid on the table.

"Go," the worker said, looking less than thrilled to be there.

From the corner of his eye, Pete could see Ava concentrating on the low, easy targets, cut out of pink, blue, and green plastic. He immediately aimed for the higher point circles. The numbers on his scoreboard shot up.

"Time."

Ava looked eagerly at her score, but her face fell at the sight of his. "Man, I thought I did well."

"Choose any prize," the kid told Pete, tossing his hand back toward the wall of plush behind him.

"You pick," Pete said to Ava.

"Really?"

"Yeah. Teddy bears aren't exactly my style." That was the truth, but not all of it. Pete was happy to be able to win Ava something.

"Thanks."

She hugged her pink bunny as they strolled through the rest of the fair's offerings, but halted at the sight of a father and son picking away at a bluegrass competition. Pete joined her for a few minutes, taking stock of the pair's red and black cowboy-style outfits.

"My dad plays the banjo," Ava spoke up suddenly. Pete looked over to see her eyes welling up with tears.

Uh-oh. Pete never knew what to do with a crying person. He put what he hoped was a comforting hand on her back.

"I thought that people only played the banjo in movies," he said.

"Don't you start with the small-town jokes," she poked a finger in his chest. "The banjo is a very hard instrument to play."

"I'm sure," he said, watching the musician's fingers fly over the strings.

"I don't suppose you like country music?" Ava sniffed, seeming to already know the answer.

"I'm sure that if I had something in common with the people who wrote it, I would," Pete said, trying to be objective.

"You like hip-hop, don't you?" Ava looked at him in judgement. She laughed suddenly.

"What?" he asked.

"I'm just picturing you bobbing your head to the beat."

"I do," Pete said gravely, happy that Ava's expression had lightened. "Up North, I wore the hood of my sweatshirt up and everything."

"You still sound like you're from the city, you know. You talk at a faster pace than everyone else."

"No I don't," Pete bristled.

"It's true," Ava said casually. "I can almost hear a rhythm to the way you talk. Especially when you're trying hard to make a point. It's cool. But it's okay to slow down sometimes, too. Enjoy life a little." She wafted in a breath of turkey-leg-scented air as if to demonstrate her point.

"I can enjoy my life not living in slow-motion," Pete shot back, realizing that he was only proving her right, that arguments often flew out of his mouth faster than thought.

He didn't like the thought of being different or out of place. But, he had to admit, it was nice to know that Ava had been watching him so closely.

# # #

The wind was making a tangled mess out of Ava's hair, but Pete didn't seem to notice. He was looking at her with warmth, and had seemed reluctant to take his hand off of her back after he had to calm her down from yet another emotional outburst.

She guessed that she was just feeling the growing pains of stagnation with her job search, plus the weight of a faltering—*don't even think about it!*—relationship. During the daily grind of work, she didn't always notice how she missed her family and her home until something came into her path like the banjo player, reminding her of all that she had left behind.

She and Pete caught up with Mariana and the group, who were pouring out of the Ferris wheel gate, still coupled, of course. Ava smiled at Mari once she noticed that Jon and her friend were holding hands.

"Ready to go?" Mari asked Ava. They had made plans to top off their day by driving into a neighboring town for an early dinner. Ava nodded, turning to Pete.

She crossed her arms, suddenly shy. "Thanks, I had a nice time."

"Thank you, for rescuing me from what was almost a boring day." His lips twitched upward, and Ava felt surprisingly sad to be leaving. "I'll see you at church," he said.

"See you."

Jon walked the girls to Mari's orange slug bug and gave Mari a quick hug while Ava looked away, judiciously studying the grass.

Once they were in the car, Ava commented, "it looks like you two had a good time."

"We did." Mari exited out of the fairgrounds onto a winding two-way road. The farther they got from Summer Shores, the more the houses spread apart until the homes turned into fields of grazing cattle.

Ava craned her head out the window. "I guess I didn't realize that Florida had farms."

"A lot of the land is orange groves. Get away from the bigger cities, and this is what you see."

"It's nice. It reminds me more of home. So..." Ava turned to face her friend. "Are you and Jon official now?"

"Yeah," Mariana beamed. "I really like him. I invited him over for dinner this weekend."

"Really?"

"My mom is so excited. She's got this whole menu planned out," she rolled her eyes. "I hope my family doesn't scare him away. Already, my brothers won't stop teasing me."

"Jon seems pretty infatuated with you. I don't think much will scare him away at this point."

"Yeah? I bet he's not expecting my dad to bring his guitar out and serenade him."

"That sounds great!"

Mariana waved this optimistic observation away. "So, what about you, was it awful being stuck with Pete all day?"

"Actually, no. We got along great."

"Really? You were just complaining about him the other day!"

"That's mostly because I was mad that he beat me in trivia. He could smooth out some of his edges, but honestly, it's nice to be around someone that you know means exactly what he says."

"Unlike Jackson?"

"No!"

Sensing the dip in Ava's mood, Mariana steered the conversation to a safer subject.

"Have you ever been to a tearoom before?"

"No."

"You're going to love it. Especially because you read all those Jane Austen books. It's called 'Something Blue.'"

"As in weddings?"

"They do a lot of bridal showers, but my mom and I have gone a bunch of times just to eat."

They pulled into a quaint little building, complete with a white picket fence.

A cobblestone sidewalk paved the way to the entrance, where the front door was painted in a glossy shade of navy. Decorative Victorian grilles graced the panes of the square windows on either side of the cottage. There was even a little garden to the side with a gazebo.

"How beautiful!" Ava said.

The interior of the building further embraced its name. There were blue saucers, teacups, and knickknacks mounted on every wall. Lace doilies laid above cerulean tablecloths. There were even blue silk ribbons on the backs of all the wicker chairs.

"Welcome to Something Blue. I'll be right with you," an authentic Englishwoman said as Ava and Mari entered. Though her face was framed by sharp lines—a square-cut bob, bangs, little black-rimmed glasses—her expression was all friendliness. She deposited a fresh pot of tea to a table of guests, and hurried into the kitchen.

Ava mouthed to Mari, "Seriously?" She knew that British people were people like everyone else, but that didn't make Ava any less in awe when she came across a person who hailed from the land of her favorite novels.

"Shall we?" Mariana asked, pointing to a stack of hats and fascinators on the top of an end table.

"We shall!"

The proprietress had hung a mirror nearby, and Ava and Mariana modeled a few different options in front of the glass.

"I love that one," Ava said, at the sight of Mariana in a cream pillbox hat. The netting fell over her black hair like an old-time movie star. She even had the red lipstick to complete the picture.

Ava picked out a purple headband with feathers and gems. They had just pouted and snapped a quick picture when the woman returned.

"Thank you for waiting," she said. "Clare" was printed on her nametag. "Is it just the two of you today?"

"Yes," Ava said.

"Perfect. Right this way."

From their small table, Ava and Mariana could look outside and see the rosebushes.

Clare handed them each a menu. "Here is our complete list of our hand-crafted, loose-leaf teas. I'll give you a few minutes to look it over, and please let me know if you have any questions."

"Thank you so much," Mariana said, skimming the menu expertly.

"I had no idea there were so many flavors of tea!" Ava said.

"I try a different one every time."

Ava studied the black teas, where adorable titles like "Wedded Bliss" preceded descriptions of what each tea was composed of. "I like a sweeter taste. But they all sound good!"

"Try 'Kiss the Bride,'" Mari advised.

"Ok, as long as I can try a sip of yours."

"Of course!"

They also ordered scones with clotted cream, tea sandwiches, and pastries. The baked goods came out as a first course, along with a pot of tea for each girl.

"I love the cozies," Ava complimented Clare.

"Thanks, they're handmade."

Bright, quilted material hugged each pot to keep it warm. Ava felt so refined as she lifted the poppy-print cozy and filled her beautiful china teacup. With notes of vanilla and raspberry, the tea barely even needed any sugar.

The scones were thick, soft, and warm, and the clotted cream was so sweet that Ava felt like dipping her teaspoon in the dish.

"I heard you picked up an extra shift tomorrow morning," Mariana said.

"Yeah, I might as well. I'm not really doing anything else."

"Are you still keeping your eye out for teaching jobs?"

"There's actually a job fair on the twenty-seventh, so I've been scanning the websites of those schools to try and decide which ones I would want to apply to. That's not for a few weeks, though."

"That's exciting," Mari said.

"Could be," Ava replied, stamping down a fit of nervousness.

Clare was timely in whisking away their scone dishes, replacing them with plates that held assorted finger sandwiches. Ava sampled the spicy crab meat one, inhaled the mild cucumber variety (feeling very English), and declared the egg salad her favorite.

When Clare set down a filigreed silver platter of cookies, jam tarts, and sponge cakes, Ava could see how all the light menu items added up to be a full meal.

She said to Mariana, "We have to make this a regular thing."

"For sure."

After the girls left their thanks and compliments with their server, Mariana saved Ava from buying up the gift shop and drove her home.

In bed that night, Ava tried to focus on the positives of the day—her goofy headband, the warm feeling in her belly after downing a whole pot of tea—but her eyes kept snapping open, her head tossing around all the possibilities of seeing Jackson tomorrow.

That's it! No more moping, she commanded herself. Ava opened up her contact list, stared at Jackson's name, and hit the call button with trembling fingers. She put the phone to her ear and counted five long rings, hanging up as soon as the phone went to voicemail.

She couldn't stand to hear Jackson's laughter-filled voice on the recording, and was afraid her own voice might shake and sound desperate if she left a message.

Staring up at the ceiling, she knew that it was going to be a hard night to sleep. She set a relaxing piano playlist on a sleep timer, and after an hour of deep breathing and sheer stubbornness, Ava finally fell asleep.

15

A hollow sense of dread had replaced the thrill of anticipation that Ava used to come into work with. Jackson was being polite but more distant than before, and she wasn't going to let him keep acting like nothing was wrong until he told her what was going on. All of that sounded good in her head, but when she walked in and found him in the break room, her courage deflated like a balloon.

"Hey, Ava!" he smiled. "How are you doing?"

"Fine," she replied lamely. *How do you start a conversation with someone who doesn't think there's a problem?* Her sense of discomfort deepened, but the feeling of frustration once he turned away and left the break room was worse. *Come on, Ava,* she told herself. *You have to do this.*

She threw her shoulders back and walked into the store, finding Jackson leaning over a register. The girl behind it—*Kaleigh?* Ava thought, trying to recall her name—threw back her coppery hair and laughed, just as Ava had done a dozen times before tonight in response to Jackson's charm.

Oh. She had suspected that the attraction he had felt for her was coming to an end, but to see such a public acknowledgement of it stung. *Did he ever intend on breaking it off with me?* she wondered. All at once, she felt nauseous.

"Hey," Kaleigh called out in greeting. When Ava neither answered nor walked away, Kaleigh asked, "Is everything okay?"

Is everything okay? Ava considered the question. *Is it okay to find the guy I've been dreaming about hanging all over another girl right in front of me?*

107

Ava stared at Jackson, unable to form light-hearted words she didn't feel.

Looking back and forth between Jackson and Ava, understanding dawned on Kaleigh's face. "Are you two...together?"

"No," Jackson said immediately. His denial was enough to wake Ava out of her stupor.

"I'm going to the bathroom," she croaked, rushing back toward the break room. Ava quickened her pace as the tears began to fall and shut herself in the farthest stall. She cupped her hand over her mouth and sobbed silently, not wanting to make a scene if anyone were to come in.

I should be happy, Ava thought bitterly. *Someone with so little consideration is not someone I want to be with anyway.* Had Jackson strung her along because he didn't want to lose her friendship? *It must have been nice to have someone fawning all over him,* she supposed. *To have someone to chat with when no one else was around.* Clearly—if he ever had—he no longer intended to start anything exclusive with her.

She tried to wrap her mind around how in the world she had let this happen to her again. Jackson's interest had felt so good, she let herself be deluded into thinking that he was genuine.

It's not that you're not good enough—she steeled herself against the insecurity which threatened to rear its ugly head at her at the thought of Kaleigh's tinkling laugh, sultry blue eyes and compact frame. *You're just not any good at deciding who's right for you.* At this bleak prospect, Ava despaired, *How can I ever trust myself again, with any decision, when I let my emotions get in the way so easily?*

The bathroom door squeaked open and Ava held her breath, frantically mopping at her eyes. She had to pull herself together. Her courtesy five-minute-bathroom break was up.

She waited until the other girl was gone and then scrubbed and dried her face at the sink. Someone would have to look extremely close to figure out that she had been crying.

She walked out to the floor, dignified, staring past Kaleigh at the offending register, and threw herself into her work with extra vigor. That, combined with the emotional toll of keeping her spirits up, left Ava exhausted as all the workers gathered in a circle for their closing meeting.

Jenny asked for the usual shout-outs and Ava, who had merely been giving the appearance that she was listening, snapped to attention when Mariana stepped forward.

"I'd like to recognize Ava. She always works hard, but not only that, she steps in to help others. She doesn't have to do that, and I appreciate it." She shot a warm smile at Ava, and it was all that Ava could do to hold back another stream of tears.

She swallowed the lump in her throat as Mari stepped back in line, joined in the applause, then gave Ava's hand a gentle squeeze.

"Thank you," Ava whispered.

After Jenny dismissed the meeting, Ava gathered her things from the cubby in the break room and held them close against her chest, as if physically willing herself to stay together until she reached the safety of her car. There, her tears flowed freely as she thought about God's providence. *How I needed Mari's encouragement today!*

She didn't understand why the Lord was so good to her, even though it felt like all she had done lately was make poor decisions, and question why he wasn't giving her what she wanted. His answer from her heart held no condemnation—only reassurance, like a warm embrace. *You are chosen, called out, and known. You are cared for and not forgotten. You are my workmanship, my child.*

"I know that I don't need anyone else!" she cried aloud. "No one but you. Help me seek no one but you." She was so tired of being hurt. Yet she knew deep within her soul that she had someone who had never let her down. Who had always been there and would never leave. And that was so much more than enough. If she could only remember it more often, if she could let the knowledge soak into her bones.

Her phone buzzed, jarring her out of her reflection. Mom. Ava gripped the steering wheel and steadied her breathing. It would do no good to be gasping and hiccupping over the phone, although she was nervous that hearing her mother's comforting voice would send her into tears again. By the second to last ring, she had got it together.

"Hello?" she said, somewhat normally.

"Hey! I have some great news!"

"What is it?"

"Mrs. Smith, your English teacher from the tenth grade, the one you liked so much? She's retiring."

Ava burst out laughing, a little slap-happy at this point. "Mom, that's terrible news!"

"No, no, she just messaged me—before she's even turning in her resignation. She wants you to take her place."

"What?" Ava had student-taught with her high school mentor, and they had stayed in touch the past few years. But she was stunned that Mrs. Smith thought that she would be a good fit to take over her life's work.

God, is this of You? "Wow," Ava said slowly.

"I know! I know you were starting to get settled down there, but doesn't this just seem perfect? Most of your other teachers are still here and could help you out for your first year. A full-time teaching job! And you had so much fun in that school...you could take over the drama club."

Ava didn't want to dampen Renee's enthusiasm, which she knew was also motivated by wanting to be near her again. And Ava missed her mother too. Yet, she couldn't commit to anything without some serious prayer and consideration.

It hadn't really ever made sense for her to come here on her own. Sure, Jess and Isaac were great, but what was she trying to do, really? Was she being practical? Maybe she should just go home. Stay where it was safe, where people knew her, could give her a hand up... she felt a renewed wave of frustration. *I can't go running home yet,* she thought. Even if the idea of being a thousand miles away from Jackson Green was extremely appealing...

Ava had no idea what she was going to do, but she wasn't going to decide anything in her current emotional state. She had committed to be here until the end of the summer, and she was going to stick it out and hope that the way would soon become clear.

# # #

At Bible study Wednesday night, Pete couldn't deny that he was looking forward to seeing Ava again. He looked up every time that someone walked through the door, but when Ava came in, his excitement fizzled out.

There was definitely something going on. Ava's eyes were red and her cheeks were flushed. She didn't look around at anyone or smile. She just sat down, pulled out her Bible, and hopped to her feet again as soon as she saw that the Wilsons had come in. Noah immediately ran over to the toy shelf in the back of the fellowship hall, and Ava followed after him and his mother.

Isaac sat down next to Pete and shook his hand. "How's it going?"

"Fine." Pete lowered his voice, "Is Ava okay?"

"I think that guy finally broke it off with her earlier today," he replied.

Pete's fists tightened. The news that Ava was single couldn't make him happy when he could see how tough it had been on her, even though he was sure that she was way better off without that punk. Pete thought, *Maybe I could go talk to her...*

Pastor Thomas came in just then from his office, where he had been talking with a congregant. It was five minutes past seven, so as soon as he sat down, he called out, "Let's get started." Out of the corner of Pete's eye, he could see Ava, Noah and Jess return.

The pastor bowed his head low and prayed, "Heavenly Father, we thank You for the privilege for coming into Your house this evening. We ask that we can focus on Your word, and that You would sustain us with it. In Jesus's name, Amen."

"Amen," Pete heard Ava echo softly.

"Please turn to Romans chapter eight, verse thirty-nine."

# # #

Pastor Thomas went over a number of scriptures on the subject of how God's people couldn't be separated from Him. Then, he had the church members close service by singing a fitting hymn called "The Love of God." Ava teared up at the title, but the tears didn't feel frantic anymore. Just cleansing. She was so thankful to God for continuing to speak words of comfort to her in her time of need, and for letting her know that she was not alone.

She had tried to avoid talking too long with anyone, but after the song's last note, Pete practically ran up in front of her to block the exit. "Ava," he asked. "Are you okay?"

It was just the question that she had least wanted to hear. She dipped her head once in answer.

Pete let out a breath. "Good."

Ava felt like she should update Pete about Jackson since he had been so good about encouraging her over the last few days. She gestured for Pete to join her on the walk outside so that there wouldn't be so many people around while they talked.

"So, you know that relationship that I didn't know whether I was still in or not?" Ava asked.

"Yeah," he said.

"I am definitely not in it anymore."

Pete caught her gaze. "I'm sorry."

"No, it's better this way. At least I know that it's finally over. That's what I wanted all along. Just not so...publicly." Ava winced at the memory.

"Hey," Pete drew her in for a hug and she buried her head in his chest. His arms were strong and warm around her. "You know, June is halfway over. Once you get a teaching job, you can get out of working with him at that clothing store."

Ava lifted her head, looking into his hazel eyes. She had never noticed how bright they flashed before. They were usually hidden behind his glasses, but they weren't at this close distance. Ava blinked a few times and stepped away, leaving Pete to drop his now-empty hands into his pockets.

"I'm not sure that I'll be here much longer at all. I just got a job offer back home."

Pete paused. "Oh. That's great."

"Yeah," Ava laughed. "It sure is. It's perfect." She didn't know what she had expected Pete to say — "Don't take it?" "I love you being here as much as you love being here?" Ava shook her head. Spiraling thoughts never gave her any clarity, and she didn't want to leave all the progress that she had just made behind the church doors.

"I'll see you later, okay?" she said instead.

"Okay," Pete smiled his small smile. "Take care of yourself."

"Thanks. I will."

Pete stayed behind, standing in the parking lot to watch her leave.

16

Ava was leaving. Pete had been telling himself this the whole time, but now that it was happening, he felt no satisfaction. Only a sickness to his core, telling him to DO SOMETHING! He had waited through Thursday and Friday morning for that sickness to go away, but now, he had had enough.

What would be the harm in asking her out? he wondered. *A little embarrassment if she turns me down? It's worth it to get this weight off of me. Besides,* his chest constricted painfully, *she'll be gone soon anyway.* He'd known Ava for a month; though their conversations had been meaningful to him, if you'd count them up, the number wouldn't amount to much. *How am I of all people going to convince her to stay?*

He drummed his fingers on the keyboard, waiting impatiently for his laptop to boot up. *Girls like letters, right? Hopefully she won't get too offended by an email.* He knew exactly what he wanted to say, and he didn't want to mess it up in a call or wait for a visit. Plus, he'd rather not get shot down in person. He typed:

Ava,

I know you're probably really busy working and all, and I don't want to bother you. But if you want to go out with me sometime, I'd love to take you. If you don't want to, I understand. I should have asked you sooner. I just couldn't let you leave without telling you how I felt.

He wanted to lighten it up a little then, so that she wouldn't feel too much pressure.

Have a great night, and I'll see you Sunday if not before.

What should I write next—yours truly? Sincerely? Pete shuddered at the thought of using either one. He settled on signing off with just his name. Send. He flexed his fingers. Now the ball was in her court.

# # #

Friday night and Ava was exhausted, but she hated going to bed right after work with no time to unwind. After a shower, she put her headphones in to watch a show on her laptop. A notification flashed— she had a new email from Pete Harrison. Ava was sure that there was a perfectly reasonable explanation for him emailing her unexpectedly at eleven o'clock at night. Still, inexplicably, her stomach tightened with tension as she clicked it open.

She must have stayed frozen, staring at the screen for a good five minutes. Reading and rereading. *What?!* Could she handle any more surprises this week?

She was surprised at the blush that flamed her cheeks. Pete was so direct in his message, and spoke so forcefully. He'd love to take her out? He just couldn't let her leave? What was she going to do? She didn't even know if she wanted to go out with him, though she was surprised at the force of her reaction after being asked. She had to act intentionally this time, and not get knocked over by flattery.

Ava texted her mom to see if she was still awake. Renee texted back right away, so Ava gave her a call.

"Mom?"

"Hey, honey! What's up?"

"I...just got asked out on a date."

"By Jackson?"

"No. Jackson and I aren't really a thing anymore. Pete asked me out."

"That teacher who you went and observed?"

Ava squinted. "Yeah."

"Oh. Well, you did sound impressed by him when we talked the other day."

"Yes, impressed by him as a professional. Do you think that I'm on the rebound?" Ava asked, twisting the end of her ponytail into a tight coil.

"No," Renee answered. "You've never been one to rush a decision. And you've always wanted to find a guy who was interested in church. But Ava, you're leaving soon."

"Yeah, about that." Ava hesitated. "I need a little more time to think about what I want."

"I thought what you wanted was a good teaching job," Renee said, sounding confused.

"I do. But I feel like I just got here, and I'm not sure that I'm ready to leave."

Ava wished that she could see her mother's face to see if her feelings were hurt, but Renee just said, "If you wait too long to get back to the school, they're going to find someone else."

Ava inhaled. "I know."

"And as for Pete—you're going to have to decide if this is someone who you think might be worth getting to know more." Ava heard Renee shift the phone away from her mouth to tell Andy, "Don't you change my station!" Ava wasn't sure, but it sounded as if her father had just got whacked with a television remote. The tension left Ava's face as she pictured her parents' familiar living room spat. Despite the inner turmoil going on in Florida, she smiled with the knowledge that, back home, some things had never changed.

"Okay, Mom. Thanks," she said.

Her mother returned to the call. "Just be honest with Pete about how you're feeling. And keep me posted!"

"All right, all right. I love you."

"Love you too."

Ava hung up, took a deep breath and pulled her journal from the top dresser drawer. She read number three from her list of dating expectations: Honesty. Being straightforward with one's intentions. She was ready to write her reply:

Hey!
Thank you so much for asking! I do want to clear something up before I say yes, though. I don't date casually. I'm looking to get to

know someone who is interested in something long-term and serious. Are you?

She could hardly believe that she hit send. *Nice going, Ava, way to interrogate the guy and question his intentions before going out on a single date!* Still, she had to hope that it was for the best. She did not want to waste any more of her heart or time.

She gripped her face in her hands, peering at the computer, and then shot up, suddenly in a hurry to put away the pile of laundry that had been accumulating at the foot of her bed. Ping! Ava dropped her folded capris and ran back to her laptop.

Pete: Yeah, I'm getting too old to mess around with that kind of stuff too. I'm serious about this.

He sounded serious. Nothing like the hassling, carefree guy she had come to know. She had seen with time that underneath his teasing exterior, there was a good heart. A heart that cared about his little nieces, an elderly church member, and her own pain at Jackson's neglect. After what had just happened to her, could she really risk breaking it, just like Jackson broke hers? *Honesty*, she thought, taking a deep breath.

Ava: I really appreciate the offer! I do want to remind you that I can't promise that I'm going to stay in the state much longer.

Pete: I know. I've been thinking about that, and I would still like to take you out if you'd like to go. We can talk about it more then.

Ava: In that case, let's meet up Monday.

Pete: Perfect. Do you like frozen yogurt? I can take you downtown. Pick you up at 11?

Ava: Who doesn't like frozen yogurt?? Sounds good!

Pete: Ok, can't wait :)

A smile emoji! Ava didn't know Pete had it in him!

She had to laugh as she remembered their very first encounter, when Pete clued Jon in on his perfect plan to woo women—his advice was to "take her around one of these touristy places, buy her an ice cream..." Ava wondered if his technique would work this time. She didn't yet know if her respect for and friendship with Pete could grow into a romantic love.

Even if she and Pete didn't hit it off, at least she would get to see more of the downtown now. She would try not to worry so much about what came after that until they had the chance to talk again.

17

Pete couldn't believe the slight tremor of his fingers on the steering wheel as he pulled into the Wilsons' driveway. He hated the nerves and discomfort of a first date. Why was he putting himself through this again? Just then, Ava emerged from the front door in a flowy blue dress with a pretty smile. *Oh yeah, that's why.*

She slid into the passenger seat and her long hair spread over her shoulder, shining gold in the sunlight. He stared for an awkward second before saying, "Hey. You look great."

"You too!" she returned. He thought that was generous, since he was wearing his normal green church polo with shorts traded in for the khakis.

"Thanks." Pete backed out of the driveway and headed downtown. "Work treating you okay?" *Could she hear the shaking in his voice? God, help!*

"Can't complain," Ava said brightly. "I'm sure you're enjoying being off for the year."

"Best part about teaching. You'll find that out soon for yourself once you start."

"Yeah," she said, looking out the window. *Great job, Pete,* he thought. *Let's kick off our date by talking about how she'll be leaving any day now.*

He changed the subject. "I don't suppose you watch any baseball?" She turned to him, indignant.

"I'm from a huge baseball family, I'll have you know!"

"All right," Pete relented with a smile. They already had church and teaching in common. An interest in sports was just an added bonus. He was spared from the fantasy of having her as a cheerleader at all his future softball games when they pulled up to Summer Shores' downtown.

Right now it only spanned about five blocks, but it seemed that every few months a new business would crop up. He hadn't really seen the appeal of a bunch of storefronts, but the place was always packed. It was clear that Ava shared in the admiration.

"I just love the history of places like these." She pointed towards a general store, "Look at that sign—it has to be fifty years old!" They drove past a grandpa buying his grandson an ice cream, and a jazz band playing for a small crowd on a street corner.

Pete parked in a space of shade on the brick-covered street. Potted plants overflowing with purple flowers hung under every lamppost— *Trying to make you feel like you were in a shaded garden instead of sweating your butt off in a glorified outdoor mall*, Pete thought. But it was pretty decent there in the winter months.

"The frozen yogurt's this way," he said. They walked side by side and he enjoyed watching Ava peer into every business's window, delighted at small bakeries, vintage clothing stores, and every kind of restaurant.

Pete held the door open for her as they reached the shop. Inside, he took a paper cup, filling it with his usual vanilla bean froyo, and chuckled as Ava studied one flavor, then another, back and forth. "You know there's going to be a test afterward," he told her.

"They all look so good!" she cried, and eventually settled on a swirl of chocolate and strawberry. "There." They moved on to the toppings. She seemed to take comfort in him dumping tons of chocolate and candy bits into his dessert and followed suit. "It's nice frozen yogurt is so healthy," she said, shaking a generous amount of those tapioca bead things into her bowl. She added a strawberry on top as if to prove her point.

"I've got it," he said, and pulled out his debit card as they approached the counter. He wanted there to be no question—this was a date. They grabbed a window seat. The chairs were hard red metal and there were goofy, multicolored dots painted all over the walls, but Pete felt anything but light-hearted. They were sitting down now, and he couldn't avoid the subject any longer.

"So, what do you think you are going to do about the job?" he asked, trying to look indifferent.

Ava pressed the bridge of her nose with her fingertips. "Honestly, I don't know."

"Have you applied around here at all?" he asked.

"They had a posting for the high school here in town, and some openings farther away where I've sent my resume in. But I haven't heard anything back yet. I can't ignore a concrete offer. A good offer," she repeated. She seemed to be talking to herself more than to him.

"I know, you should consider it. Pray about it. I can wait." Pete took a deep breath. It wasn't easy for him to open up, but he couldn't mess around now. He was out of time. "I'd like to keep seeing you while you decide, if you'd like that also. Maybe even if you do go back, although I hope you don't." *I might as well lay it all on the line*, he thought. "I've never had this much hope before."

Ava looked at first astonished, and then tender, as if she were looking at a wounded puppy. He shook his head. "Listen, I don't want that to come out wrong. I don't want to put any more pressure on you. I know we haven't known each other that long, and I'm not saying that you're my last chance or anything." *Even if you are...* his mind sourly added.

"I've dated a girl just to have a girlfriend, and it was a big mistake. What I mean is that there's something really special about you. I'd like to keep getting to know you, however long that may take."

"However long?"

"However long."

"You know in the Bible, Jacob worked for Rachel for seven years." Ava leaned back and crossed her arms, considering him.

"I don't mind working for you. Are you going to keep me waiting seven years?"

Her eyes glinted with humor. "I guess we'll have to see!"

Ava still had some frozen yogurt to finish up and there were other customers waiting to get a table, so they went outside to walk a few circles around the huge fountain in the town square. She sighed. "Do you really think I can be a good teacher?"

Pete said without hesitation, "I know you can."

"How? You haven't known me long."

"No. But I have a pretty good sense about people. That's another teaching skill. Let me ask you this. Have you ever failed at anything in your life?"

"Yes," Ava said gravely.

"Okay, name something."

"Umm," she fidgeted a moment, then huffed out a breath. "Nothing comes specifically to mind, but you put me on the spot."

"Next question. Does anyone not like you?"

"Yes. One of my neighbors back home—she hates me! I was responsible for taking care of her house when she went on vacation, and I forgot to turn the water line off. The plumbing leak cost her a bunch of money. I tried to ask for forgiveness, but I couldn't fix things."

"Wow. One whole person had a plumbing leak a couple of years ago. Listen. You work harder than anyone I've ever seen. Everyone I know who has a brain in their head loves you, and you still walk around like you don't know that you're different than anybody else. All of these things tell me that you can do any kind of work that you set your mind to. And, by the way, you wouldn't be right out of college with a job offer if your old administrator didn't also think that that was true. The only one who thinks that you can't do it, for some strange reason, is you."

Ava seemed to be grasping at further protestations, but he had out-argued her. Her expression softened in appreciation. "Thanks."

"And if you ever get into trouble and need some advice from a cranky second-grade teacher, you know who to call."

"I might take you up on that," Ava said, crushing her paper container and tossing it into a nearby wastebasket.

Pete was reluctant for the date to end but knew that she had a lot to think about. On the way back to the car he said, "Thank you," and he really meant it. "This is the most comfortable date I've ever been on."

"Me too," she said, flashing a gorgeous smile.

"Would you like to go out again sometime?" *Here it comes,* he thought. *She'll say, "Sure. Maybe sometime."*

"Does Saturday work for you?" she said, and relief flooded into Pete's chest. "I'm working an early shift, so I'm free in the evening."

"Saturday is perfect," he answered. "I know a place." They had had fun today, but he would take advantage of the later hour to show her a nicer time out. He reflected that it might be one of the few times that they had left.

He wanted Ava to do what was best for her, but secretly he prayed that their days together would go on and on. *She's got to stay here. She just has to.* And he would do everything in his power to try and convince her.

18

Friday night, Isaac watched the baby so that Jess and Ava could have a much-needed girl's night out. At the later hour, the downtown's ambiance transformed from beautiful and bright, to ethereal and romantic. The lampposts were wrapped in strings of white twinkle lights, casting a warm glow onto the sidewalk.

"I don't know what's going to happen tomorrow," Ava told Jess as they walked toward the restaurant. "When I read my Bible, I don't see: 'Ava, you should give Pete a chance.' Or 'Ava, break it off.' 'Move back,' or 'stay here.' Every option has pros and cons—I just feel lost."

"Try to be patient," Jess replied with uncharacteristic moderation. "You'll find your way. Besides, the fun is in not knowing. In living through God's plan for you."

"It's not fun if you mess it up!"

"You won't," Jess said with the infuriating confidence of a person who had experienced all that Ava had not. "You'll make mistakes, but God will give you grace, and bless you with more wisdom and clarity in time. I know that he has good things planned for you."

"I thought Jackson was good." Ava said honestly. She believed God's promises, but it was hard to overcome her feelings of doubt.

Jess acknowledged, "I was wrong to encourage you so much about Jackson. I know I have to stop being so pushy. Even if you were really happy when you came home from your date with Pete."

"You're ridiculous!"

"Old habits die hard," Jess shrugged.

Ava guessed that it was Jess's job as her best friend to always hope the best for her. And to remind her that though one guy had been bad, their God was always good.

They passed a drugstore on the right and Jess halted.

"I should get Noah some more of his lotion while we're here. He gets bad dry skin and this stuff is the only thing that works. Do you mind?"

"Go ahead. I'll wait for you here," Ava gestured to a bench at the center of the town square. She didn't mind at all to have a moment to drink in the rich scenery. Jess ducked into the store and Ava sat down in front of the fountain, which was illuminated from within. Spotlights drew attention to the bright hibiscus plants which surrounded the water.

A familiar voice called her name and she whirled around, neck prickling. *Jackson.*

"Hey, stranger," he called, reaching down for a hug. *He was actually reaching down for a hug.* Ava scooted away, and he gave her a puzzled look.

"Hello," she said stiffly.

"You look great tonight," he said.

"Thank you." Ava did not return the compliment. "I'll see you at work."

She bent over to pull her phone out of her bag, as if she just remembered that she had something critically important to do, but felt a hand fall on her shoulder. She immediately shrugged it off.

"Is something wrong?" Jackson asked her.

"Yes, something is wrong with you," she burst out, leaping to her feet. "I don't know what your problem is, that you think it is completely fine to lead me on and then flirt with other girls in front of me, but I am not okay with it. We are co-workers, Jackson. And to be honest, I'm not even comfortable being your friend anymore when you say things like how great I look when you have no intention of dating me!"

"How do you know I have no intention of dating you?" he questioned, crossing his arms.

"Let me say this very clearly so that you can understand. It is not acceptable to chase after two people at the same time. Are you telling me that you are not interested in Kaleigh?"

For once Jackson seemed speechless. He stared over her shoulder, seeming to consider her words, and Ava laughed. *At least he's finally being honest.*

"I didn't make you any promises," he said at last. "I took you out and we had some good times. I even bought you a present for helping me with my essay. I thought we were friends, so I guess I'm just a little surprised at the way that you're acting."

"At the way that I'm acting?" Ava ran her fingers through her hair. She felt like she was talking to a crazy person. "You don't see how I would think that a guy buying me expensive jewelry would be some sort of promise?"

Jackson's stance remained firm. "I thought that a beautiful girl might appreciate a beautiful gift, that's all. I can't explain the way I feel about Kaleigh. There's just something about her that I can't put my finger on."

Ava felt like she'd been slapped by a wave of cold water. She didn't know why Jackson's rejection had to hurt so bad, even when she knew that she wasn't interested in him anymore.

Jackson read her expression. "Not to say that you're not a great girl," he backpedaled. Ava shook her head. *Déjà vu.*

"You're so thoughtful, and patient," he continued, taking a step forward. "That's why I hoped that you would understand." He reached out and put his thumb beneath her chin. "Do you know how cute you are when you're angry?"

She slapped his hand away and asked, "What am I, your pet?"

Jess appeared in the drugstore's doorway and Ava breathed out a sigh of relief. "I have to go," she said. "What we had is over. So stop trying to get it back." The words sounded hollow to her own ears. Of course what they had was over. Jackson had made that abundantly clear. But she was over being confused, and she hoped that her hurt at being unwanted would soon catch up with her bold words and disappear.

Jess was looking at them curiously. "Are you good?" she asked.

Ava gave her a curt nod and stalked forward in the direction of the restaurant, with head held high and adrenaline pumping. *I am worthy of respect. I am loved. I am strong,* Ava's thoughts hummed. *Good things are coming my way.*

"Hold up!" Jess cried, her short stride taking double steps to catch up to Ava's victory march. "Please tell me you told off that jerk!"

"He shouldn't be bothering me anymore."

"You go, girl." Jess grabbed Ava's arm. "Wait, this is it! The Pink Peony. The highest-rated Chinese restaurant in Summer Shores."

"Have you been here before?"

"Yeah. Isaac and I checked it out on a date once, but it was more my style, not his. Yet another reason why I am so glad to have my best friend back!" She shoved her newly-bought lotion, tightly wrapped in a paper bag, into her tiny crossbody purse and led the way in.

The soft tones of a dulcimer welcomed them in like a wave of gentle water. Delicate potted orchids sat on openings in the wall while thick green leaves draped the columns in between. In the entryway, a small waterfall bubbled over smooth stones. It was a haven, tucked away from the bustle of downtown.

"I love it."

"I knew you would," Jess gloated.

The hostess sat them at a table adorned with hand-painted teacups and soup bowls. She wore an embroidered silk dress with cap sleeves, a high collar, and knotted buttons.

The floral theme extended to the menus, which were printed with a rosy-pink border. Jess naturally gravitated towards a dish with three flame icons next to it. After some waffling, Ava settled on the sweet and sour chicken.

Their server, who was also wrapped in a lovely silk qipao but in a darker shade than the hostess's, promptly appeared to take their order.

"Welcome to the Pink Peony," she said, pulling a pad of paper out of a small satchel. "My name is Zoe. Is this your first time dining with us?" The teal color of Zoe's dangling earrings shone under the dining room's dim lighting.

"It's my first time," Ava said. "It's so beautiful here. I love your earrings, by the way."

"Well, thank you twice," the young girl said. "The restaurant is a family business, and the sea glass jewelry is my business."

"That is so impressive! Do you have a website?" Ava asked.

"I sure do." Zoe produced a business card.

"Thanks, I will definitely check it out." As Zoe left for the kitchen, Ava thought about how many remarkable people she had met here and of the new places she had gotten to see. Jess and Mari were not making Ava's decision any easier by continuously showing her all of Florida's finest establishments.

Jess poured herself a cup of tea. "Sweet and sour chicken? Really?"

"Don't judge," Ava said. A few minutes later, she was vindicated by an entrée which was a hundred times fresher and more delicious than her grocery store favorite. Pink Peony's version was not as sugary sweet, but was brimming with flavors like ginger and onion.

"Has your mom texted with any updates about your sister?" Jess asked.

Ava nodded. "I mean, it could be false labor again, but at least the hospital is keeping her for observation this time." She had been so distracted by Jackson's appearance earlier that she hadn't checked her phone for a while. She pulled it out and gasped.

"Ava?"

"She's here! Hope Tamryn Byrne. 7 pounds, 2 ounces." Her eyes misted and she flipped her phone around to show Jess. "She's beautiful."

"Aww! So tiny and sweet! Julianne looks happy."

The tears escaped Ava's eyes, leaving twin wet trails down her cheeks. She dabbed at them with her cloth napkin and stirred sweet and sour sauce through her rice without taking another bite.

Jess leaned forward and took her hand. "Are you okay?"

"Of course, I'm thrilled. Everyone's healthy. It's just..." she took a deep breath. "I'm not there." She looked up. "I want to hold her, Jess! I want to take my own pictures and hug my sister and give Hope her stupid teddy bear in person."

"Go for a visit," Jess suggested.

"It won't be the same. She'll be a month old by the time I build up enough days off." Ava shifted in her chair. "How much more of her life am I going to miss if I stay away from home?"

"I'm sorry, Ava. I know this is hard." Jess paused, searching for the right words. "Isaac and I had to sacrifice a lot coming here. The place that we met. Moments with our families. But it was where our future was, and I wouldn't trade the new memories we've made for anything. I'll keep praying that you'll have peace as you try and make the right choice for you."

"Thanks." Ava sniffed and straightened out her shoulders. "Now let's enjoy this dinner. I should be celebrating. I'm an aunt!"

"Yes you are, and I can already tell from the way you are with Noah that you are going to spoil that girl to death."

"You bet I am!"

Ava had a growing sense that the stakes kept rising while clarity receded. Still, Jess's friendship and promised prayers helped.

She texted her sister a quick congratulations, put her phone away, and determined to absorb the tranquility of her surroundings.

19

Twenty-four hours later, when it was time for her second date with Pete, Ava was less than tranquil. Sitting in Jess's passenger seat, she pulled at the edge of her peach cap-sleeved top, making sure it laid just right. She ran her fingers through her hair, shaking it loose where it caught on her heart-shaped gold pendant necklace. She checked her lip gloss in the sun visor's mirror.

"Relax, you look great," Jess said, grinning.

"Thanks. And thanks for dropping me off."

"No problem, it was on my way. And Pete's going to take you home?"

"Yep," Ava said.

"If anything changes, just call!"

"I will. You're the best."

Jess's shoulder lifted jauntily. "I know."

Ava hopped out of the car and waved to Noah as Jess drove away. She perched herself on a stone bench since she was still several minutes early. The restaurant soared impressively above her with "Ellis Seafood" emblazoned in block letters at the top. Peeking through one of the windows, Ava could see candlelight twinkling on tables covered with white linen.

She let out a low whistle and turned forward, not wanting to be caught gawking. She didn't have to wait long before Pete arrived.

"Hey," he said as he walked up the sidewalk. Ava hoped she hadn't imagined it, but she saw there was a lightness to him, a broadness to his smile that she hadn't seen before. She had noticed the change during their date Monday, and now again today. She turned her attention from his newfound enthusiasm to his dark jeans and button-down shirt.

"You clean up good!"

He shrugged that off, but said, "You too."

Pete opened the door and they went inside to give the host his name. Tonight, Pete was polished, the picture of politeness, but there seemed to be a slight discomfort about it that she actually appreciated. He was steady, real, and it gave her a sense of calm that she'd never felt with a guy before. She found herself replaying his words from earlier in the week—*I'll work for you.*

Ava jarred herself back to the present as the host escorted them to their table. He propped up tall, hardcover menus next to each of their place settings, and embarrassed Ava slightly by pulling out her chair and placing a napkin on her lap. "Please let me know if you need anything, and your server will be right with you," he said, folding his long fingers in front of him.

"This place is really nice," she told Pete after the host left. Her crystal goblet was filled with ice water, and Ava thought she would be more than happy to just have that to drink—*even the water here is fancy!*

"Yeah, I know it's a little over the top, but the food's amazing. Good for a special occasion."

"Well, thank you for bringing me," Ava said, flattered that Pete considered dining with her to be a special occasion. She opened her menu, staring at the rows upon rows of entrees. "Wow. What are you getting?"

"Their house special."

She looked at the long list of fish included under the special, not wanting to admit that she wasn't the biggest seafood fan.

"Ava?" she looked up and realized Pete had asked her a question.

"Sorry. I get kind of focused in on one thing and tune out everything else. I can be really absentminded sometimes!"

Pete furrowed his brow. "Don't be so hard on yourself. Being able to focus sounds like a good thing to me."

"I guess I never thought about it that way. It can make things a little awkward, though. I remember one time in high school, I walked into a wall because I was thinking so hard before a history test."

"It happens to the best of us," Pete said.

"And then I apologized to it."

Pete grimaced. "Okay, that is pretty bad. Were there a lot of people around?"

"Thankfully, no one that I was close with." Ava appreciated Pete's sympathy, but she couldn't imagine him ever wandering around without direction, or bumping into anything. He always walked with brisk purpose, and had the bearing of a linebacker.

Their waitress arrived, and Ava ordered the baked tilapia, figuring she'd like all the grilled veggies.

Pete repeated his earlier question— "So, what's new since I've seen you?"

"Well, I have a job fair to go to on Monday, and an interview at Summer Shores High on Wednesday."

"That's great."

"And I have to give my principal back home an answer by Friday."

Pete winced. "No pressure."

"Yeah, I know." Ava drew her pointer finger down the cool surface of her water glass. "Oh well, I guess I'm lucky she gave me that much time. I'm just praying that I'll make the right decision."

"Whatever's meant to happen will happen. That's the way it was when I found my job. It's just hard when you're going through it."

"Either way it will be such a big change. But I know I'll be okay."

"You will," Pete said, resting one elbow on the back of his chair.

Ava's expression brightened. "And, my niece was born last night! Do you want to see a picture?"

"Sure."

She dug out her cell and froze at the sight of the text on her screen.

Jackson: Ava, I know you think I've been acting like an idiot, but I really do care about you. I think you're pretty and funny and smart, and I loved the time that we spent together. I've been thinking about what you said. Maybe it was selfish of me to hold onto you when I was falling for someone else, but I couldn't bring myself to let you go completely. If it makes you feel any better, Kaleigh heard that we

131

went out a few times and doesn't want anything to do with me now. I'm going to try to win her back though. I hope that we can still be friends?

Ava dropped her phone on the table so that she wouldn't be tempted to text back right away. It was funny how Jackson had a justification for every one of his actions in his "apology."

"Who is it?" Pete asked, though his grim expression hinted that he already knew. "Not *him* again?"

"Yup," Ava's voice quavered from the heat of her anger. "The poor guy got dumped by the girl he ditched me for."

"Want me to beat him up?"

"No," Ava smiled and Pete grinned in return. "I'm not going to let someone like him wreck my night. He clearly has issues that he needs to work out."

"You can only control yourself," Pete agreed. "Some people need to get smacked around by life a little bit to figure out how to be decent on their own."

Being across the table from a supportive friend took some of the sting out of Jackson's latest level of blatant inconsideration. Ava knew that she had to stop living her life held hostage by choices that other people made. She had to grow closer with givers like Pete, and distant from the takers like Jackson who seemed to be perpetually drawn to her. She prayed a quick prayer—*Lord, I know that you have a better plan for me than what I thought Jackson and I had. Help me to forgive him even though he hurt me. Thank you for protecting me, even though this is hard.*

Could a relationship with Pete be a part of God's better plan? Ava didn't know—she couldn't rest on that. But she could rest in God and the constant that He provided as she walked ahead.

Their waitress returned, lifting some of the heaviness that had intruded upon the evening. Pete raised a pitying eyebrow as the girl slid Ava her small, single plate before unloading Pete's colorful cornucopia of dishes. But Ava knew that the fish and zucchini she ordered would fill her up enough.

"Let me know if you want to try any of this," he said, gesturing to his feast.

"I've never had lobster before. Or crab."

"What? And you ordered tilapia? You have got to try some of this." He fixed her a little plate, and she studied the crab legs suspiciously.

"Here, watch me." He broke one open with practiced hands and swung the meat around in a dish of butter.

Ava tried to replicate his technique—usually she was a quick study, but she wasn't used to having to put in so much effort for her food. Plus, as she had admitted to Pete earlier, her coordination wasn't always the best. Her hands slid pitifully on the tough shell and Pete reached over to demonstrate again.

She picked up a second leg and splattered crab juice on herself with a shriek, but she had broken in! Pete's shoulders shook with laughter. Ava wiped her arm with as much dignity as she could muster and took a bite. Her mouth puckered in surprise.

"Mmm, this is really good!"

"Yeah, it is!"

"Thanks for making me try something new."

Pete wiped his mouth with his thick napkin. "Hang around with me, and you'll be surprised how much your palate will expand."

"Maybe next time you can make the food," Ava said. *Would there be a next time?*

"I'd be honored."

Between the lobster tail, the crab legs, and her tilapia, Ava was stuffed. The waitress brought Pete the check, and Pete waved away Ava's efforts to help pay, though she was sure the final bill was expensive.

As they were leaving, Pete lingered near the exit. "Do you want to go for a walk?" he asked.

"Sure, that sounds nice." It had cooled significantly since night fell. They walked along a metal railing, which was lined on the other side with tall shrubs. The pathway was almost deserted.

Just then, a red firework exploded right above them, shimmering on its way down. *Really?* Ava thought. *There are literal fireworks on this date?* She and Pete stopped to watch some more illuminate the darkness. Someone in the bordering neighborhood must have started their Fourth of July festivities early.

When she first moved down to Florida, Ava never would have believed that she would be here with Pete. "You know, I wasn't sure if

I should go out with you at first," she told him.

"No, you're joking!"

"I told your sister-in-law Amber that we didn't seem like a logical match."

Pete thought for a moment. "I know that we don't. But we have the important things in common. We have the same values and the same direction. And, to tell you the truth, I'm glad you're not a loudmouth like me."

Ava started to protest his self-depreciating humor, but he said, "No, really. That's what I'm encouraged about. You have strengths that I don't, and my deficits aren't yours. That's why this can work. Unless you're just trying to tell me that you're sorry you ever agreed to go out with me."

"I'm not sorry," she laughed, and she meant it. Was she scared that it wasn't going to work out between them? That their growing friendship couldn't last the circumstances and miles that might try and separate them? Yes. *But I'm not sorry for tonight.*

"I won't be sorry either, whatever you decide. I've really enjoyed getting to know you." His expression belied his casual tone, and she dropped her eyes at the intensity of his gaze. She was not going to kiss a guy on the second date! Especially one she might have to leave behind in a week's time.

Looking heavenward, she instead took him by the hand, and drank in the perfection of the moment. As another firework shot across the night sky, she thought about how small she really was, and how thankful she was to be able to count on God to bring her these flashes of light.

20

Ava's behemoth of a purse snapped open as she dropped it by her feet in Pete's passenger seat. This exposed a cell screen, dotted with missed calls and messages from Jackson Green. "Seriously? Take a hint," she said, rapidly swiping away the notifications until her eye caught on one of the texts.

Jackson: I know this is a real jerk move but I didn't know who else to call. I need your help.

"Jerk move," Ava thought sardonically, *the man is capable of introspection.*

She braced herself, hoping she wouldn't regret opening the conversation. When she scrolled back up to the first message, she gasped, turning to Pete. "Jackson's in the hospital! He got in a car accident."

Pete's hand froze above the ignition. "And he's texting you about it?"

"His parents are in Iowa, and I'm pretty sure the only friend he ever mentioned to me, he made up to get out of a date."

"It sounds like he deserves to be alone."

Ava looked at Pete, shocked. "The accident sounds bad. He needs help, whether or not he deserves it."

Pete rolled his head around in irritation, then said, "Fine. But I'm coming with you."

"You might just want to take me home to get my car. It could be a late night. I'm going to pick up the key to his apartment so I can take his dog out and make sure that it's fed."

"Let me get this straight—Jackson desperately needs you... to babysit his dog?"

"Yes," she eyed him. "I hope you were kidding about the whole 'beat him up' thing you said earlier. He already got t-boned."

Pete grimaced. "That is rough. All right. I still want to come and make sure you get home okay, but I'll do my best to keep my mouth shut."

"Thanks."

Ava's fingers turned white from gripping her phone as they turned into the hospital. Light from the streetlamps gleamed over three stories of glass.

"Did he say what room he was in?" Pete asked.

"105." They hustled across the mostly-full parking lot and made it past security. The woman at the front desk printed their visitor passes, and scanned them in through a set of double doors to the right. Pete wrinkled his nose. The hallway smelled of bleached laundry. The nurse responsible for the east wing hopped to his feet.

"Can I help you?"

"We're here to see Jackson Green," Ava said. "Can we go in?"

"Sure," he said, leading the way. "I was going to check on him soon anyway."

They turned the corner to see Jackson with one leg propped up and iced. Cuts sliced over the pink beginnings of bruises on his skin. His head was wrapped in a bandage, and he was hooked up to an I.V.

"Jackson," Ava breathed. "What happened?"

Jackson broke into his signature grin, although she could tell that the movement caused him pain. "I ran a red light. Stupid, right?"

"Very."

"It's worse than it looks," Jackson said as the nurse shined a light from eye to eye. "They're keeping me overnight to watch the concussion, and then I should get to go home."

"How's your leg?" the nurse asked.

"I'm starting to feel sore again," Jackson said.

The man made a few marks on Jackson's chart. "I'll be back with some more pain medication."

Ava watched as Pete, still hovering near the exit, moved to make way for him. She had forgotten that Pete was even in the room.

"Jackson, this is my friend Pete. He drove me over."

Pete gave a curt nod of acknowledgement, and Jackson took in the couple's attire.

"It seems like I ruined your night."

"Not at all, we were leaving the restaurant!" After a glance back at Pete, Ava figured she should add, "But we had a great time."

"I guess you'll be wanting that apartment key," Jackson said, shifting incrementally to his right side and reaching over.

"Wait, I'll get it! Where is it?"

"On top of the seat," Jackson said, tilting his head toward a paisley-patterned armchair.

Ava snapped open the transparent plastic bag labeled "Patient Belongings," fishing Jackson's key ring out of the bottom.

"It's the gold one with the apartment number on it. When you get to the gate, you'll need to sign in with the security guard."

"Security guard?" Ava asked, eyebrows rising.

He nodded. "When you get in, the kitchen is to the left. Duke's food is on the bottom shelf of the pantry, and his bowls are close by. Leash is hanging by the door. He's not shy of strangers, so he should be all right."

"Okay, I'll take care of it. You're supposed to be discharged tomorrow?"

"Yes."

"So you'll be needing a ride?"

"Yeah. And if you could check on Duke in the morning also..."

"Sure. You probably need some groceries too? How long are you going to be laid up?"

"My knee's not broken, but I have a torn meniscus. I should be getting around better in a week or so, but until then, I'm supposed to stay at home."

Ava nodded.

"Thank you so much." Jackson's eyes brimmed with relief. "I knew I could count on you." He turned to Pete, "And thanks, man."

"Don't mention it." Pete asked Ava, "Ready to go?"

"Yeah." She gave Jackson one last pitying smile and turned away.

Pete was silent all the way to the car. When they got in the vehicle, he turned to her. "Why did you let him work you over like that?"

"What are you talking about?"

"He treated you like garbage your whole time here, and suddenly you can't do enough for him?"

Ava's voice rose in response to the accusation in his tone. "I'm choosing to help someone who needs it," she said. "That is not being 'worked over.'"

"He's using you."

"I feel bad that he got hurt. Don't you?"

"You've got to stop caring so much about what happens to everyone else." Pete stabbed a finger in her direction, saying, "That's when people take advantage of you, and get you to do whatever they want."

He started the car and drove toward the apartments.

"Do you even know where we're going?"

"Yes!"

They fell silent. Ava had a keen sense that she had disappointed Pete, and she didn't know how. The thought burned inside of her. "Is that what you think of me? That I'm a pushover? That I'm stupid?"

"You think that I'm a jerk who has no clue what he's talking about. Do you want to know what I think of you? I think that you can be a stronger person, and you choose not to because it's easier to get people to like you by working yourself to death."

"You have no right!" Ava cried. "You don't know me at all. You're just so cynical that you can't imagine wanting to do something nice for someone else."

"I'm here tonight, aren't I?"

"Yes, ruining everything!"

"You know what, Ava? I'm sorry I messed with your and Jackson's plans. I thought things were different between us."

The statement rang with bitterness and hit Ava like a punch in the gut. In other words, he had thought *she* was different—from all the other girls he had known, all the people who had disappointed him. But she wasn't. She could feel her hold on the night's joy breaking, and her thoughts scrambled for something solid to cling to. *I was made good. I can't lose God's love, I cannot lose it.*

She swallowed hard. "I'm sorry you feel that way," she said stiffly. "I thought you were different too." Shouldn't she have known? Shouldn't she have known that someone so calloused couldn't possibly be for her? *He's not calloused,* she thought. *You just let him down. Why can't you act better?* Warm tears started spilling down her face and she hugged her arms. She turned away to face the window.

They pulled into the apartment complex. The individual buildings, painted white with black trim, towered above the gates toward the dark sky. She peeked over as Pete pulled into the security station and filled out some particulars on a clipboard. The guard took his driver's license to scan. *Intense,* Ava thought.

When they were cleared, they drove on through the complex's amenities, which had been previously blocked by the interlocking tree branches that shaded the front entrance. The length of a gigantic, zero-entry pool spanned four buildings, dotted with gauzy cabanas. Tennis and beach volleyball courts were visible further in the distance. Pete followed a series of signs which directed them to the apartments numbered in the 400s. Each building had its own spacious parking lot.

They soon discovered that each building also had its own spacious lobby. Ava's awe overcame her pride momentarily as she told Pete, "I feel like I'm in a hotel." They passed a water wall and pool table on their way to the elevator, their steps echoing over the swirled taupe tiles in the abandoned room. The walls were paneled in teak wood, leading up to a vaulted ceiling with a candelabra.

The tension between them was harder to ignore as the elevator door closed, boxing them in. The soft instrumental music which floated down from the speakers only highlighted their silence. From her peripheral vision, Ava saw that Pete was leaning against the side railing, staring straight forward.

The elevator dinged. Ava darted out and down a beige-carpeted hallway. After a little struggle with the lock, which she refused to ask for help with, she opened room 408.

Jackson had his own *foyer.* The entryway, decorated on either side with nondescript oil paintings, led into a massive living room with a fireplace.

That's practical for Florida, Ava scoffed, but even she couldn't deny the space's beauty. It was modern, sleek, and hardly looked lived-in. As the door slammed shut behind them, Ava heard the tinkle of a collar, woofs, and pounding feet. Duke launched himself around a corner and onto Ava's legs, his pink tongue wagging.

"Hey, there." Ava tentatively dug her fingers into his soft fur. "Aren't you a handsome boy."

Duke was a gray-and-white husky with startlingly blue eyes. "Don't worry, buddy," she told him. "We're here to take care of you."

Duke barked in the direction of the door. "I'll take him out if you want to stay here," Ava said to Pete.

"Nah, I'll go with you."

Part of Ava dreaded an extension of the awkwardness, but she couldn't deny that, at the late hour, she was glad to have someone along. "Ugh," she said, spotting a poop-bag dispenser at the side of the door, next to the leash.

"You can do that part, though," said Pete. Sensing a mild truce had been reached on terms of necessity, Ava's lips twinged in the hint of a smile. She clipped the leash onto Duke's collar, trying to steady the bouncing dog.

"Listen," Pete said, keeping his voice low as Duke bounded down the public hallway. "I didn't mean to attack you. I've had some bad experiences with trust in the past."

"And you don't think you can trust me?"

"No, it's not that." They got in the elevator, and Pete gripped his forehead, trying to explain. "I'm not good at being patient, or communicating things in the best way. When I see something that's wrong, nine times out of ten, I'm going to point it out. But that doesn't mean that I don't care about you, or that I think any less of you." The elevator descended. "You know that I think the world of you."

There was his way again, of making her close her mouth and think, even though minutes before, she had been fuming. He didn't use grandiose statements often, unlike Jackson, whose compliments dripped from his mouth every other sentence. But when Pete did use them, it mattered. "Okay," she said simply.

"Okay?" he repeated.

She nodded as the doors opened. They exited to the grassy lawn to let Duke do his business, and walked him around the lot a few times.

"All of this high-class stuff doesn't make me feel better about this guy," Pete said, shoving his hands into his pockets. "Like he doesn't have enough going for him."

"Jackson's got plenty going against him too," Ava reminded him.

"Do you want me to go with you to pick him up tomorrow?"

"Nah, I'll be all right. I'll probably run by the store after church, and hopefully he'll be discharged by then."

"That's good of you," Pete said charitably.

"And he should be able to manage by himself after that." Ava knocked Pete's elbow. "There's only one guy that I want to be spending all my time around."

"Does this guy have a two-hundred-foot pool?"

She took his hand for the second time that night. "No. Just a sweet heart and a killer chicken pot pie."

# # #

Outside of the hospital the next day, a nurse helped Jackson out of his wheelchair. The two struggled for a minute to comfortably maneuver his leg—now secured in a brace—into Ava's vehicle. Jackson thanked the nurse and buckled up as Ava pulled out of the pickup lane. "How are you feeling?" she asked.

"Not bad." Jackson turned to take in the paper bags covering Ava's backseat. "Thank you for all this, and for picking up my prescription."

"No problem."

He clasped his hands in his lap. "I can't wait to see Duke. Was he good for you?"

"He's the sweetest. He'll be happy to see you."

Jackson stared at the dash. "It's good to know someone would have missed me if I was gone."

"Don't be ridiculous. What about your parents?"

"They're not home enough to notice the difference between me being there, or in Florida, or across the ocean."

"Are you still going to do your volunteer program?" Ava asked.

"Yeah. I've got a physical therapist scheduled to come by a couple times a week, so I should heal up by the time I'm supposed to fly out. And I hired a driver, so you won't have to come and get me again after today."

After a short silence, Ava said, "Do you want to talk about what happened?"

Jackson's face was, for once, devoid of humor. "I saw headlights coming my way, and the next thing I knew, medics were pulling me out of my twisted car. I blacked out for minutes. I could have died."

"I'm sorry," Ava said.

Jackson's head dipped low. "I don't know why you're still being nice to me, Ava. I hope I didn't mess things up between you and that guy."

"We're fine. I hope things work out for you, too."

"I don't deserve it," Jackson said without hesitation.

"It's never too late to change," Ava reminded him gently. "I may not be a manipulator —" Jackson winced at the label. "But I have my own issues to work through. And I believe, that it's the trying that counts."

As the two pulled into Jackson's palatial housing complex, even amidst luxury that Ava could never dream of affording, Ava felt sorry for him.

21

Ava walked up to a butter-yellow high school gym for Monday night's career fair, clutching a black folder containing a dozen copies of her cover letter, resume, and references, as well as work samples from her student teaching. She had even memorized an audio recording of herself, practicing an introduction over and over again until her "elevator pitch" sounded put-together, but natural. She had been interviewed before at Hydrangea and for a campus office job, but this was far more pressure—this was for her career.

Despite her preparations, nothing readied her for the sight of hundreds of other applicants lined up when she opened the door. As she stepped inside to wait along with the others, Ava anxiously studied the map that she printed off of the job fair's online registration page.

She had drawn purple stars in the squares which designated where the schools that she was interested in would be sitting, and she had even double-checked the list with Pete to make sure that her research-driven conclusions were correct.

Slowly, the line crawled from the lobby to the gym, where the schools had set up their tables in rows. The sound of dozens of simultaneous interviews reverberated against walls that were covered with green athletic banners.

The man in line in front of Ava appeared to be roughly her age, and she struck up a conversation with him to pass the time. His name was Anthony. He moved here from Georgia. No, this wouldn't be his first teaching job, and it wasn't his first job fair, either. Ava looked self-consciously from his sharp black suit, shiny shoes, and confident smile to her own attire. She hoped that her navy skirt, cardigan, and ruffled blouse weren't too casual.

She checked in at the front table, and then she was free to roam wherever she wished. Of course, it looked like all of the schools that she had scoped out online had small lines forming in front of them already.

Her first stop was the table for Washington High School. She hung back at a respectful distance and tried not to listen in as the interviewee in front of her chatted, laughed, and altogether sounded competent. Ava stepped forward for her turn, and a man and a woman in matching orange polos greeted her. Her throat was suddenly dry, and she envied the pair's coffee cups and water bottles.

Ava wasn't quite sure what to expect, but after she told them a little about herself, things proceeded much like a normal interview: "Why are you qualified to take this position?" and so on. A string of endless meetings followed, punctuated by a couple memorable spots—one lady asked her to imagine, if she were a fruit, what kind would she be?

"Pardon me?" Ava asked the woman.

The interviewer's butterfly-wing earrings swung back and forth over her periwinkle tunic as she leaned forward, eager to know Ava's response. "You know, a fruit. Would you be a persimmon? Mango?"

"I guess I would be an apple?"

She leaned back. "I see…"

Making her way to the last stop, Ava tried to paste on a smile over her exhaustion—the final table belonged to a charter school with great national rankings.

The woman seated behind a hand-chalked school sign was impeccably dressed, with golden hair strands blended through the tips of her dark brown curls. She looked up from typing the interview notes from her last candidate on her laptop.

"Hi there," the woman leaned forward to shake Ava's hand. "I'm Candace Johnson."

"Ava Keller."

"Please, have a seat," she extended her hand towards a folding chair.

144

"Thank you. I saw you have an opening for an English teacher?"

"Yes. Specifically, twelve-grade British literature. Do you have any experience in that subject?"

"My concentration in college was British literature!"

"But no experience," Candace said, flicking her glossy red fingers through Ava's resume.

"Unfortunately, no. I worked with ninth and tenth-graders in my student teaching, but I'm a hard worker, and a fast learner."

Candace smiled and nodded politely. "Who would you say has most influenced you?"

Finally, something that's easy to answer, Ava thought. "As I'm getting older, I've found a lot of inspiration from my grandmother. She had this strength about her, like she knew who she was and she wasn't trying to be anyone else. I hope to emulate that kind of assurance in my own career."

"That's nice." Candace referenced her notes. "How would you evaluate students other than by tests?"

"I would give them a menu of project options that help them play to their strengths. They could turn in artwork, a speech, or a piece of writing—as long as they demonstrate knowledge of the concept."

"Hmm," Candace smiled, and Ava thought, *this woman would be a killer poker player.* "What kind of extracurriculars would you be interested in running?" she asked.

"The drama club," Ava replied. Candace seemed to be waiting for more. "I could do any kind of academic club, really. No athletics, though!" she smiled hopefully, and Candace looked mildly amused.

"Got it. Last question—tell me about a time where you have successfully managed a classroom."

"Uhh..." Ava said expressively. "I can't say that I've managed students by myself before, but I did pick up a lot of tips from my mentor about proximity, positive relationships, pacing..." she threw off as many classroom management buzzwords as she could remember.

"Thank you for meeting with me, Ava. Your interview was great, but I just don't think you have the amount of experience that we're looking for at our school. Please feel free to reapply once you have a few more years under your belt."

Ava's heart sunk, but she said, "Thanks so much for the opportunity." As she turned to leave, she saw the guy that she had made small talk with when she first came in, sitting at the next table over with the lady who asked Ava the fruit question.

Anthony must have had a heck of an answer, because before Ava passed by, she saw them shaking hands, and witnessed the interviewer bending down to pull a contract out from a box of files. Anthony caught Ava's eye and grinned. "Good luck," he whispered.

"Thanks," she waved, thinking that she couldn't get out the door fast enough.

No one had offered her a job, and it seemed like the principals who gave her the most positive feedback were the representatives from the schools that she least wanted to be at. The hope that she had held for her upcoming Summer Shores High interview evaporated. It seemed like for every position that she came across, there were plenty of seasoned candidates standing by, ready to take her place. The summer was ending, and so were Ava's options.

22

Ava felt sick to her stomach as she pulled into Summer Shores High School, and not just because of her impending interview. She glanced at the clock—3:45—*Enough time to freak out a little before I head to the conference room.* Everything was making her mournful lately—the warm summer sun filtering through the majestic oaks on her drive to work, the white blooms dotting the waxy leaves of the magnolia tree in Jess's front yard, even the fresh tomatoes in the lunch line at church —leaving her to wonder, *Can I really walk away from all of this?* Pete's warm smile flashed through her mind, and she pushed the image away to focus on the task at hand.

Perusing the school website last night, she confirmed what Mariana had told her—Summer Shores could be a great fit. Their mission statement, "to provide a diverse multitude of learning opportunities to support the well-being of every child" was posted over a slideshow of smiling teens in soccer jerseys, students carving in woodshop, and friends posing in the cafeteria. One image had particularly appealed to her inner poet: a science experiment being conducted on the front lawn. She could picture herself bringing her own students outdoors to read on a nice day.

With a deep breath, she headed for the administration building. The secretary let her know that the principal was expecting her and would meet with her shortly. Ava took some time to look over the front display. It seemed that the joyful environment which the school had captured online wasn't just good publicity. Here in the office, they had printed the senior portraits of last year's graduating class—enough to paper the whole wall—along with a line from each student about their self-reported future plans. Some of the graduates had instead sent in a kind note about who or what they would miss from their time there.

Behind the front desk, the secretary had adorned the wall with shelves holding colorful flowers, candles, and even a framed Bible verse painted in deep purple script—Isaiah 40:10: "Fear thou not; for I am with thee." Any nerves Ava was feeling dissipated at the reminder. She was where she was supposed to be. At least in that moment, she could find peace to meet with these fine people. She could leave knowing that God could see what was ahead and was working in her favor. No matter what happened.

"Miss Keller?" A suited man with graying hair appeared from behind a side door. Dr. McCoy, the principal. He gave her a warm smile and extended his hand. She shook it firmly and followed him in. She was thankful to see it that would just be him and her seated at the wide wooden table—the idea of a panel interview had always made her nervous.

Ava settled into a cushy office chair and offered Dr. McCoy her folder. He opened it and glanced over her resume for a moment before asking, "What made you want to get into education?"

"I always wanted to be in a job where I could help people, but as a teacher, I also get to share my love for books," she said.

He gave her an appreciative nod. "I see you've been working for the same company for the past six years."

Ava, recalling her years of interview training in college, tried to make her response relevant to education. "It's given me practice connecting with a lot of different people every day, and experience in time-management because we are usually pretty busy."

"As a teacher, time-management is definitely essential since you'll only have fifty minutes per class period. Could you walk me through a sample lesson you would teach?"

Ava took a deep breath and remembered an activity that went over well while she was student teaching. "I would start the lesson with a thought-provoking question. For example, if I was teaching a sonnet to high-schoolers, I would probably ask them something about love or poetry to get them thinking about the topic. Then, I would explain the structure of the sonnet. I would break the poem down into smaller parts and assign one part to every couple of students so that they could study it for form and meaning."

Passion infused Ava's voice as she pictured the "lightbulb" moments she had so loved to provide for the students. "I think that a lot of times, kids don't like English because they don't feel that it is accessible to them. But if they focus on one chunk that's not too overwhelming, they can see that it is possible for them to understand!"

"Absolutely." Dr. McCoy leaned back and studied her. "Now, what would you say are your three biggest strengths and weaknesses?"

Ava groaned internally. She had always dreaded this question in an interview. First, she had to make sure that she didn't sound like she was bragging; then, she had to make sure that her terrible qualities weren't so terrible that she wouldn't get hired for the job.

"Well," she paused. "I'm really organized, and I care a lot about other people. I feel like I'm a good listener. Because I care so much, I guess my biggest weakness would be that I can let that get to me. I can be a perfectionist, and I'm very concerned with what others might think. Was that three..." she trailed off. *Ugh, I am so not getting this job,* she thought.

Dr. McCoy waited politely until he realized that she could think of nothing else to say. "I think I've heard all I need to," he said.

Ava rose immediately. "Thank you so much for the opportunity."

"Wait a moment, Ms. Keller," he held up a hand. "Please, have a seat." Ava nodded, too nervous to speak.

He continued, "I knew from the resume you sent in with your application that you would be qualified for the position, but I needed to meet you in person to know for sure. We won't be interviewing anyone else. The job's yours, if you want it."

Ava's mouth fell open in pure, unadulterated shock.

"Please give us a call by the end of the week with your decision," Dr. McCoy said. "At that time, Mrs. Silva will tell you more about the fingerprinting and paperwork that you need to do. I hope to be hearing from you soon."

"You will," Ava said with a smile she could no longer keep down.

As she walked to her car, Ava was relieved to discover that this choice felt simply right. It was like everything leading up to this day—all of the failures and the victories—had been perfectly orchestrated to let her know that this was the place where she belonged.

She drove to Bible study still in disbelief. She didn't know why. She professed to believe in a God who could work amazing things on her behalf. She guessed that she simply hadn't had the faith to feel sure that He would do it in her own life. As awe-inspiring and all-powerful as God was, he was also her friend and father. It was a good thing that she didn't have to rely on her own understanding of what was possible.

She looked at the clock and deflated a bit. Her mom would be off from work by now. It was time to break the news to her.

Ava asked her phone's voice assistant to call home and put the call on speaker.

"Hello?" Renee answered.

"Hey Mom," Ava said.

"How did it go?" Renee asked cautiously.

"I got the job."

"That's great! But what's wrong? You don't sound very excited."

"I know you want me to come back home."

"I do want you to come home. I miss spending time with my baby girl. But you're all grown up now, and I have to trust that I've prepared you to live your own life. I would never want to keep you from a place where you're happy, because that's all your dad and I have dreamed for you. Are you happy, Ava?"

She grinned. "I really am." *Happy, free, complete.*

"Then that's what matters. Don't worry about us. Now I have an excuse to get your father to take some time off so we can come visit you!"

Ava laughed. "That would be great! Thank you."

"We love you, sweetie, and we are so, so proud."

"I love you too. I'd better let you go—I'm almost to church."

"Say hi to Pete for me," Renee teased.

"Yeah, yeah." As Ava hung up the phone, she felt that one final weight had been lifted. She was always so concerned about not letting anyone down. Her family's support just went to show that she didn't need to worry about anything.

Her breath caught as she saw Pete pull in at the same time she did. In her sudden distraction, she did a horrible, lopsided parking job but was thankful to at least have made it between the lines. Ava returned his smile as they both exited their vehicles. "Hey," he said.

"Hey."

"So, how'd it go today?" Pete asked casually.

Ava burst, "You're not going to believe it. The principal offered me the job on the spot!"

He leaned against his car and grinned. "I'm not surprised."

"I mean, I barely have any experience! He said that he really connected with my enthusiasm for learning when he first read my cover letter. What are the chances of there being an opening at the best school in the area, right at the time when I need it?"

"Pretty amazing." He looked at her expectantly.

"Oh! I guess you want to know if I'm going to take the job?"

"I'm waiting with bated breath," he answered wryly.

"Yes! You know, it's crazy, I was really expecting a 'don't call us, we'll call you' sort of thing."

"Wait," Pete put a hand out to stop her rambling. "So, just to make sure, you're not going home?" he asked.

She paused, trying to form her emotions into words. "I know it's strange, but Summer Shores feels like home now too. I can't go back when God is blessing me so richly here. A piece of me would be missing. I'd be cutting off the growth I have seen in myself, and always be wondering what would have happened if I stayed."

"You're not going to change your mind on me, now?"

She shook her head. "I'm not going to pretend that I'm not a little scared, that there won't be a small part of me whispering, can you really handle all this change? But I don't have to do it alone."

"No, you don't." Pete took her by the hand, and she could see relief sweep over his features. He would have been shaken if she had brought him other news tonight, she could tell, but he had put on a brave face for her. His fingers tenderly swept her hair back from her cheek, and it made her feel like someone treasured.

She reciprocated in force, throwing her arms around him movie-style and not caring about what heads would turn their way.

# # #

Ava was his, and Pete had no words to express how good that it felt. Ava was staying where he could hold her and look after her. Pete hugged her tightly in his arms, breathing in the flowery scent of her hair. Then, he lifted her up a second time and gave her a spin for good measure. At the sight of her pretty face framed by the pink sky, Pete couldn't help but think, *Amber was right. I am turning into some kind of romantic hero.*

The hesitation and sorrow that had so often plagued Ava's expression were gone, and the happiness which replaced them was so radiant that Pete let her down gently and leaned in close.

"Are there any rules against kissing a church girl on the third date?" he asked her.

"Hmm..." Ava tapped her lips, thinking. "I'm pretty sure that it's frowned upon in most situations."

In that moment, Pete recalled a relevant argument that he had thought up back at the church barbeque. "There are exceptions to every rule," he told her.

Ava gripped his sleeve and said, "Stop being a know-it-all and kiss me." Pete needed no further encouragement.

Their lips met and Pete knew without a doubt what he had been denying for years now. He wanted and needed a woman to spend his life with. But not just any woman. "Ava."

He allowed himself to say the name out loud that he had spent weeks trying to banish from his thoughts. He would stand by her and give her all the time that she needed until she could see what he had already concluded—that they were absolutely meant to be.

Ava might have been brought down to Florida for a job, but Pete liked to think that maybe, just maybe, God had brought her for him. And when he thought about all the items on his memorized list of blessings, Ava completely blew the rest of them out of the water.

Pete looked behind her when he heard tires crunch over the pavement. "Let's go inside and face them all at once," he said. It would be refreshing not to have to run and hide from their friends' interference anymore. Elizabeth Allen, Pastor Thomas, Jake, Amber, and Isaac would all be thrilled to see that Pete and Ava's idiotic avoidance of one another had changed to affection.

"Oh my," Ava's jaw slackened when she saw the owner of the green sportscar that had pulled into the lot. "It's Jackson."

Pete's muscles tensed automatically, but when Jackson limped out of the passenger side of the vehicle, he looked right at Pete and gave him a hesitant smile.

"I'm not here to cause any trouble," he said. "I was wondering if Ava's invite to come to Bible study still stands?"

Ava beamed. "Of course. Don't you know that church invites never, ever expire?"

"Even when the invited person is a horrible sinner?"

"Especially when the invited person is a horrible sinner. You'll fit right in with the rest of us. Come on."

Pete had thought that he was pretty much an expert on human nature, but Jackson showing up surprised him. He guessed that the accident had shaken the kid up. Or it could have been Ava's act of goodwill afterward.

Ava dragged Pete close by her side as she hustled forward, guiding Jackson up the sidewalk to make him feel welcome. Pete shook his head at the thought that he had been coming to Summer Shores Church for more than a decade, and, yet, Ava was the one acting like she owned the place. But he loved it.

# # #

Kaleigh Taylor wrung a bottle brush through her son's sippy cup as she thought about the past week at Hydrangea. Work had been nice and calm since Jackson had been out. She heard he'd been in a car accident. *Good riddance.*

Kaleigh had felt so ashamed when she saw Ava run away from her register two weeks ago. She didn't know the girl well enough to feel comfortable chasing her into the bathroom, so instead she stayed behind to confront Jackson. He admitted that Ava may have got the wrong idea about their relationship status, and that was all Kaleigh needed to hear. She didn't have time for any more liars and cheaters in her life.

She had been wary of men ever since Aaron's dad left her. Since him, there had been a handful of others who just wanted to pick her up for a night of fun. But she wasn't that girl anymore. She was a mother with responsibilities. And, after Ava's outburst, the sweet memories of Jackson hanging around and joking with her had turned to vinegar in her mouth.

Of course he's just like the rest of them, Kaleigh thought.

153

Sure, there were times where she was down on her knees at the end of the night—so exhausted that she felt like her head could explode—that she wished she had a shoulder to cry on. Someone to help lift her burdens.

But the thing was, guys weren't interested in grocery shopping or cleaning up accidents. They weren't big fans of women with wounds from their pasts. They were only interested in how she could brighten up their present.

No, she would not allow anyone to get close to Aaron. And she would certainly not allow an overgrown child like Jackson Green to get close to him.

She quickly rinsed the plastic cup and laid it out to dry as she heard her baby calling for her—Aaron was awake from his nap. He was her world and her life, and she didn't need anyone else.

# # #

August came, and, with it, pre-planning week for school. Ava sat through orientation, professional development classes, and technology training. She found all of her new colleagues to be friendly and welcoming. Finally, the time came for her to enter her classroom for the first time.

Ava fiddled with the key, overcome with the gravity of the moment.

"You got it?" Pete asked, barely visible behind his armload of furniture—he was carrying her newly-purchased butterfly chair and a floor lamp with bendable heads back from her college days.

"Yeah, sorry." She unlocked the door and turned on the lights.

The room was decently sized and freshly painted. The students' desks were in rows, and behind them was her very own desk and chair. "You can put those down over there," Ava told Pete, pointing to the front corner of the room.

Pete made a second trip back to the car to gather up her framed literary quotes, featuring all the greats from C.S. Lewis to Alfred, Lord Tennyson. Ava had searched for hours online to find the perfect posters—she wanted her walls to breathe out a love of reading.

Pete was a champion, not complaining as he unloaded the six substantial boxes of used books that would form the beginning of her classroom library.

She squeezed his arm. "Why don't you go and grab a cup of coffee?

I'm okay here."

Pete kissed her cheek. "Okay. I'll see you in a bit."

He left and Ava took a seat, unsure of where to begin. There was so much to do. And so much that she had never done before.

She closed her eyes. At this point, the old Ava would have broken down with fear. But experience had taught her better. *God* had taught her better.

There was no magic cure for gaining confidence, maturity, or peace. She simply had to open her eyes to the love that He had placed all around her. Pete, Jess, Mari—they had all helped her so much. They were a part of her story, as was everyone who had shown her kindness as she walked along a way that was, at times, unsteady.

She had to embrace the whispers of grace that she'd been fighting and make them become her truth. Then, she would be able to offer back what she had been given with a settled heart. She was called, but not to save the world. Not to do it all, or do things perfectly. She was called to be His child.

She didn't yet know how she would manage six classes of twenty-five teenagers each—if she could reach them, or make them listen to what she had to say. She didn't know what she was going to teach on the first day, or the first week. She didn't know how to turn on her projector or run the copy machine. But Ava knew that she would get there. God had gotten her this far, and he would carry her the rest of the way.

She blew out her breath, unable to procrastinate any longer. Starting small, Ava unpacked her office supplies, and the more she handled the brightly colored pens and the textbook that she would be working with, the more she thrilled with anticipation for the days to come.

"God," Ava prayed aloud, "I'm ready now."

Epilogue

One Year Later

Ava stood with her father in the hallway that ran perpendicular to the doors of the church sanctuary. Andy, who was dressed to the nines in a gray suit, squeezed Ava's arm gently when he noticed her breathing pick up. *What in the world do I have to be nervous about?* she thought.

She was marrying the man of her dreams—the day that she had waited for for so long had finally arrived. She had no reservations about her choice in groom. Pete brought out the best in her, loved her to death even before taking his vows, and would fulfill every duty to her with the faith that he let shine through all of his daily responsibilities.

Her solemnity was more due to the fact that she was pledging before God to take care of this precious person. To do right by him, unconditionally, forever. She hoped to always embrace the power of God's spirit within her to accomplish this heart's desire that, for once, was not born out of fear, but of love.

Ava knew that the Lord would be with her through this next chapter of her life, because He had already fulfilled His promise that He "is able to do exceeding abundantly above all that we ask or think." Looking back, she marveled at how sustaining God's presence had been as she waited for Him to knit together the precious pieces of her story.

"You look like a princess," Andy leaned in to tell Ava, the laugh lines beside his eyes crinkling.

"Thank you, Daddy," she said, and kissed his stubbly cheek.

Julianne stood in front of them, draped in rose-pink chiffon. Her tea-length dress had a sweetheart neckline that matched Ava's own gown, and she held a handful of white lilies, the petals of which contained just a pop of bubble-gum color. Julianne had dropped right back to her tiny, original size after having Hope, and Ava, after hanging out with the two of them this week, could understand why.

Even now, Juli struggled to chase after Hope in her satin-ribboned heels once she noticed the infant toddling after the two other flower girls, Rose and Ivy. The older kids were running circles around each other and scuffing up their white patent-leather shoes. Ava didn't care. This day wasn't about perfection. It was about celebration.

Amber swooped in to the kids' rescue so that the matron of honor could hug her sister and make her way down the aisle. Then, Amber steered the little girls into formation, handed them three identical, petal-filled baskets, and sent them on their way.

Ava stepped forward and peered around the hallway corner. Inside of the sanctuary, white gauzy pew bows had been fastened to the ends of the rows. Sparkling, sheer fabric had been sheathed over the hand-carved archway where Pete awaited her. She ducked her head back when she saw Pastor Thomas raise up two jubilant arms, telling the congregation to please rise.

This morning, Jess had curled Ava's long hair into loose ringlets, pinning up half and making her feel like a woodland fairy. She even wore a glittering silver circlet above her veil to complete the enchanted picture. Although the styling and adornments made Ava feel dazzling and special, their charms were nothing in comparison to the soaring joy she felt from within.

As the music changed and first few notes of "Be Thou My Vision" flooded the church, tears of thankfulness pricked Ava's eyes. How far God had brought her. As Jon and Isaac, their ushers, held the doors open for her grand entrance, she didn't worry about stumbling over the sequined butterflies embroidered on the hem of her elegant gown. She only briefly took in Pete's brother standing across from Julianne at the front of the sanctuary.

As she locked eyes with her soon-to-be husband—who was

laughing because he was just too contrary to cry tears of joy like a normal person—as she looked toward her future, her love, and her blessing, she raised her voice to sing along with the rest of the congregation:

> Riches I heed not, Nor man's empty praise;
> Thou mine inheritance, now and always;
> Thou and Thou only, first in my heart,
> High King of Heaven, my treasure Thou art.
>
> High King of Heaven, My victory won;
> May I reach Heaven's joys, bright Heaven's Sun!
> Heart of my own heart, whatever befall,
> Still be my vision, O Ruler of all.

THE END

Acknowledgments

Thank you to God for making all of my dreams come true and then giving me a new one. You are faithful and true, providing in every time of need. I understand now more than ever that all beautiful and imaginative things are from You!

Thank you to everyone who welcomed and inspired me at the beginning of my adult life—all the brothers and sisters in Christ who have succored me in my spiritual walk. Your kindness and guidance means the world to me.

Thank you Dad for printing out all my papers, and Mom for editing them—for your tireless support and the solid foundation you gave me. Thanks to Noreen for the help babysitting!

Thank you Kyla, Moriah, Robin, Zelma, Julie, Sofie, Lois, and Tori for reading my drafts and providing kind feedback. Thank you to Mike Constantino for my beautiful website! I have had so many people cheering and praying for me, and I know I could not have done this without you.

Thank you to my editor Savanna Roberts for patiently teaching me the elements of a strong novel and for your direction in growing the story. Also to Katie for passing Savanna's information along! The Christian writing community is so wonderfully supportive, and I am thankful to have learned from excellent authors and agents via blog posts and AFCW workshops this year.

Thank you to my husband for creating a legendary love in my heart and stability while I write. Thank you to my children for bringing me

159

new light, joy, and wisdom daily.

I am truly so blessed to have each of you in my life. Thank you for reading my story.

About the Author

Rachel Blanchard is a teacher, wife, and mother of two young children. She received her Bachelor of Arts in English at Truman State University in Kirksville, Missouri before moving to Central Florida. She is passionate about sharing lessons learned, and the message that we can trust in God's goodness. If you enjoyed this story, please connect with Rachel at www.rachelblanchardwriter.com, or leave a review!